出差英語

一把罩

國家圖書館出版品預行編目資料

出差英語一把罩 / 張瑜凌編著
-- 二版 -- 新北市：雅典文化，民106.08
面； 公分. --（行動學習；12）
ISBN 978-986-5753-87-0（平裝附光碟片）
1. 商業英文 2. 會話
805.188   106010060

行動學習系列 12

出差英語一把罩

編著／張瑜凌
內文排版／王國卿
封面設計／姚恩涵

法律顧問：方圓法律事務所／涂成樞律師

總經銷：永續圖書有限公司   CVS代理／美璟文化有限公司
永續圖書線上購物網   TEL：（02）2723-9968
www.foreverbooks.com.tw   FAX：（02）2723-9668

出版日／2017年08月

 雅典文化

出　22103　新北市汐止區大同路三段194號9樓之1
版　　　　TEL　（02）8647-3663
社　　　　FAX　（02）8647-3660

搞定出差英文，快速提升職場競爭力！

　　到國外出差時，最害怕遇到什麼情形？恐怕是雞同鴨講的溝通問題吧！明天臨時要到國外出差，英文又不是非常靈光，該怎麼辦呢？「出差英文一把罩」幫您解決所有出差可能遇到的溝通問題！

　　「出差英文一把罩」涵蓋八大單元：在機場、出境、投宿旅館、電話聯絡、和客戶互動、會議、簡報、商展，提供您最精簡、實用的《精選例句》，以及《精選句型》的文法分析，讓您可以更快速瞭解句型結構的用法；再搭配相關單元的《單字整理》，以方便您查詢相關單字。

　　想要單槍匹馬到國外出差搶訂單嗎？想要讓公司高層對你刮目相看嗎？想要在國外商展中和客戶優質互動嗎？「出差英文一把罩」助您一臂之力，讓您在國外出差的商旅過程中，順利完成使命！

Chapter 1　在機場 Airport

Chapter 2　出境 Departure

Chapter 3 投宿旅館 Hotel

Chapter 4 電話聯絡 Phone

Chapter 5 和客戶互動 Client

Chapter 6 會議 Conference

Chapter 7 簡報 Briefing

Chapter 8 商展 Trade Show

DATE: 10-03-12 FLIGHT: 501 WEIGHT: 3

1578-52

UNIVERSAL
AIRLINES

Athens

WORLD
AIRLINES

FLIGHT 504

VALID ONLY ON THE DATES AND FOR
THE FLIGHTS SHOWN ON THE TICKET

MOSCOW

195004

FLY GROUP
AIRLINES

1406   021 B

FLIGHT: 203   WEIGHT: 10

213-551

在機場
Airport

訂機位

精選例句

→ I'd like a nonstop flight[1].
　我要訂直達的班機。

→ I want to fly to Chicago on the 1st of September.
　我想要在九月一日飛芝加哥。

→ I'd like to book[2] flight[3] 803 on August 25th.
　我要訂八月廿五日的803班次。

→ I'd like to book a nonstop flight from New York to Paris.
　我想預訂從紐約到巴黎的直達航班。

→ I'd like to book the first flight to Seattle for May 1st.
　我想預訂五月一日到西雅圖的最早航班。

→ I want to make a reservation[4] from Taipei to Seattle.
　我要預約從臺北到西雅圖的機票。

→ I want to cancel[5] my reservation.
　我想取消我的訂位。

精選句型

I'd like~

我想要~

句 型

I'd like +
| to + 原形動詞 |
| 名詞 |

※ I'd = I would

句型範例

❖ I'd like to make some friends from the USA.
我想要交一些來自美國的朋友。

❖ I'd like a cup of coffee.
我想要喝一杯咖啡。

Word Bank

1. nonstop flight 直飛班機
2. book v. 預定
3. flight n. 班機
4. make a reservation 預約
5. cancel v. 取消

Unit
2

航班查詢

精選例句

→ Do you fly[1] to Seattle?
你們有到西雅圖的航班嗎？

→ Do you fly to Seattle on next Monday?
你們有下星期一到西雅圖的班機嗎？

→ Do you fly to Seattle on September 2nd?
你們有九月二日到西雅圖的班機嗎？

→ Could you please find[2] another flight before it?
能請你找在那之前的另一個班機好嗎？

→ Are there any seats available[3] on the 2 pm flight?
下午兩點的飛機還有任何空位嗎？

→ Could you check the boarding time[4] for me?
你能替我查班機時刻表嗎？

→ How often do you fly to Seattle?
你們有多經常飛西雅圖？

在 機 場 **Airport**

（精選句型）

Could you please ~?

能請你~嗎？

句 型

Could you please + 原形動詞 +
| me |
| us |
| him/her |
| them |

句 型 範 例

❖ Could you please send me this book?
能請你寄這本書給我嗎？

❖ Could you please tell her where to take a taxi?
能請你告訴她去哪裡搭計程車嗎？

Word Bank

1.fly v. 飛行

2.find v. 尋找

3.available a. 可用的、有效的

4.boarding time 班機時刻

003

Unit
3

特定航班

精選例句

→ I'm looking for[1] a flight to Paris on July 3rd.
我正在找七月三日到巴黎的航班。

→ I'm planning to depart[2] on September 1st or 2nd.
我計劃九月一日或二日出發。

→ Are there any flights to Paris that arrive before noon?
有沒有可以中午以前抵達巴黎的班機？

→ I'd like to reschedule[3] the flight at 4 pm.
我想把班機改成下午四點的航班。

→ I want to leave[4] on next Wednesday.
我想要在下星期三離開。

→ I'd like to change the flights for the same date.
我想改成同一天的其他航班。

→ I'd like an earlier/a later flight.
我想要早一點/晚一點的班機。

在機場 **Airport**

I'm looking for~

我正在找~

句 型

I'm looking for + 名詞

句型範例

✤ I'm looking for a job.
我正在找工作。

✤ I'm looking for a new monitor.
我正在找新的螢幕。

✤ I'm looking for my daughter.
我正在找我女兒。

Word Bank

1. look for 尋找

2. depart v. 起程

3. reschedule v. 重新安排日期

4. leave v. 離開

Unit
4

確認機位

精選例句

→ I'd like to confirm[1] my seat.
我要確認我的機位。

→ I'd like to reconfirm[2] a flight for Mr. Lee.
我想替李先生再確認機位。

→ Do I have to confirm my flights?
我需要確認我的班機嗎?

→ When should I confirm my flights?
我什麼時候要確認我的班機?

→ How should I confirm my flights?
我要如何確認我的班機?

→ My name is David Lee.
我叫做李大衛。

→ My name is Mary Jones, that's
M-A-R-Y J-O-N-E-S.
我的名字是瑪麗 • 瓊斯,拼法是 M-A-R-Y
J-O-N-E-S。

在機場 **Airport**

精選句型

Do I have to ~?

我需要~嗎?

句 型

Do I have to + 原形動詞

句型範例

❖ Do I have to do something different?
我需要做一些不一樣的事嗎?

❖ Do I have to give up?
我需要放棄嗎?

❖ Do I have to call him?
我需要打電話給他嗎?

Word Bank

1. confirm   v. 確認

2. reconfirm   v. 再確認

005

Unit 5

辦理報到

精選例句

→ Check-in[1], please.
我要辦理登機。

→ I'd like to check in.
我要辦理登機。

→ Can I check in now?
我現在可以辦理登機嗎？

→ Can I check in for CA Flight 546?
我可以辦理 CA546 登機嗎？

→ Can I check in for my companions[2]?
我可以幫我的同行的人辦理登機報到嗎？

→ Where can I check in for CA Flight 546?
我可以在哪裡辦理 CA546 班機的登機？

→ What time should I have to be at the airport?
我應該什麼時候到機場？

→ How early[3] can I check in for my flight?
我可以多早辦理登機報到？

在機場 **Airport**

精選句型

Check-in, please.

我要辦理登機。

句型範例

❖ I'd like to check in.
我要辦理登機。

❖ I checked in 2 hours before departure.
我在離境前二小時辦理登機。

❖ I checked in my baggage the day before takeoff.
我在起飛前一天辦理登記我的行李。

Word Bank

1. check-in 辦理登機

2. companion n. 同伴

3. early adv. 提早地

006

機位安排

 精選例句

➜ Can I have a window seat[1]?
我可以要靠窗戶的座位嗎？

➜ Can I have a window seat near to the lavatory[2]?
我可以要靠近盥洗室的靠窗戶座位嗎？

➜ I don't want the aisle seat[3].
我不要走道的位子。

➜ I want an aisle seat, please.
我想要一個走道的位子。

➜ I want an aisle seat in the smoking section.
我要吸菸區靠走道的位子。

➜ Is it an aisle seat?
這是靠走道的座位嗎？

➜ I'd prefer a non-smoking seat.
我要非吸菸區座位。

➜ I want the first class seat[4].
我想要頭等艙的座位。

精選句型

I'd prefer ~

我寧願要~

句 型

I'd prefer +
| to + 原形動詞 |
| 動詞 ing |
| 名詞 |

句型範例

❖ I'd prefer to meet you at your office.
  我寧願在你的辦公室和你見面。

❖ I'd prefer having your help.
  我寧願要有你的幫助。

❖ I'd prefer a cup of tea.
  我寧願要一杯茶。

Word Bank

1.window seat 靠窗座位

2.lavatory 盥洗室

3.aisle seat 走道座位

4.first class seat 頭等艙座位

MP3 007

Unit
7

行李托運

精選例句

→ I have baggage[1] to be checked.
我有行李要托運。

→ I have two suitcases[2].
我有兩件行李箱。

→ How many baggage can I check in?
我可以攜帶幾件行李？

→ How many baggage can I take on a
China flight?
搭乘中國航空的班機我可帶多少行李？

→ Can I carry this bag with me?
我可以隨身帶這個袋子嗎？

→ Is there a weight limit[3]?
有重量限制嗎？

→ How much is the extra charge[4]?
超重費是多少？

→ What are your charges for excess[5]
baggage?
你們的行李超重費是多少？

在機場 **Airport**

精選句型

How much ~?

~是多少？

句 型

How much +

be 動詞 + 主詞
助動詞 + 主詞 + 動詞

※ much 形容不可數名詞

句型範例

- ♣ How much is it?
  多少錢？

- ♣ How much did you ask?
  你說要多少錢？

Word Bank

1.baggage　n. 行李

2.suitcase　n. 小型旅行箱

3.limit　n. 限制

4.extra charge　超重費

5.excess　a. 過量的、額外的

008

Unit
8

行李提領

精選例句

→ Where can I get my baggage?
我可以在哪裡提領我的行李？

→ Is this the baggage claim area[1] from USA Airlines 702?
這是美國航空702班機的行李提領處嗎？

→ Can I get my baggage now?
我可以現在提領我的行李嗎？

→ Could you help me get my baggage down?
你可以幫我把我的行李拿下來嗎？

→ Where can I get a baggage cart[2]?
我可以在哪裡找到行李推車？

→ Where is the baggage cart?
哪裡有行李推車？

→ Excuse me. That is my baggage.
抱歉，那是我的行李。

→ This is not my baggage.
這不是我的行李。

在機場 **Airport**

精選句型

Could you help me ~?

你可以幫我~嗎?

Could you help me +
原形動詞
with/about + 名詞

句型範例

* Could you help me move it into the bedroom?
可以幫我把這個搬進臥房嗎?

* Could you help me with this box?
你可以幫忙我(搬)這個盒子嗎?

Word Bank

1.baggage claim area 行李提領處

2.baggage cart 行李推車

Unit
9

行李遺失

精選例句

→ I've lost my baggage.
我遺失我的行李了。

→ I don't see my baggage.
我沒有看見我的行李了。

→ One of my bags hasn't come.
我的一件行李沒有出來。

→ Did you see my red bag?
你有看見我的紅色袋子嗎？

→ Where is the Lost Baggage Service[1]?
行李遺失中心在哪裡？

→ Do you know where the Lost Baggage Service is?
你知道行李遺失中心在哪裡嗎？

→ I think two pieces[2] of my baggage have been lost[3].
我覺得我的兩件行李遺失了。

→ How long will you find out?
你們要多久才會找到？

在機場 **Airport**

精選句型

Do you know where ~?

你知道~在哪裡嗎?

句 型

Do you know where +

> 人 + be 動詞/一般動詞
> to + 原形動詞

句型範例

* Do you know where he is?
  你知道他在哪裡嗎?

* Do you know where to find it?
  你知道在哪裡可以找得到嗎?

Word Bank

1.Lost Baggage Service 行李遺失中心

2.piece n. 件

3.have lost 已經遺失

MP3 010

Unit
10

轉機

精選例句

→ I'd like a stopover[1] flight.
我要訂需要轉機的班機。

→ I'd like a stopover flight to Seattle.
我要訂到西雅圖的轉機班機。

→ I prefer to stop over in Hong Kong.
我比較喜歡在香港轉機。

→ Where can I get information on a
connecting flight[2]?
我可以到哪裡詢問轉機的事？

→ How should I transfer[3]?
我要如何轉機？

→ How should I transfer to Paris?
我要如何轉機到巴黎？

→ I'm in transit[4] to Paris.
我要轉機到巴黎。

→ I'm connecting[5] with CA651.
我要轉搭 CA651 班機。

在 機 場  Airport

How should I ~?

我要如何~？

句型

How should I + 原形動詞 / be 動詞

句型範例

* How should I get there?
  我要如何到哪裡？

* How should I be your friend?
  我要如何成為你的朋友？

Word Bank

1.stopover　n. 中途下車(轉機)

2.connecting flight　轉機班機

3.transfer　v. 轉機、轉車

4.transit　n. 過境

5.connect　v. 連結

Unit
11

過境

精選例句

→ How long will we stop here?
我們會在這裡停留多久？

→ How long is our layover[1] in Seattle?
我們要在西雅圖停留多久？

→ How long is the stopover[2]?
過境要停留多久？

→ Do I need to change planes?
我需要轉機嗎？

→ May I leave[3] my baggage in the plane?
我可以把行李留在飛機上嗎？

→ I'm a transit passenger[4] for Flight UA706.
我是要搭乘 UA706 航班的轉機乘客。

→ I'm continuing[5] on to Los Angeles.
我要繼續前往洛杉磯。

在機場 **Airport**

精選句型

How long ~?

~多久?

句型

How long + | 助動詞 / be 動詞 | + 主詞

句型範例

* How long did you spend?
  你花了多少時間?

* How long are you going to stay here?
  您要在這裡停留多久?

Word Bank

1. layover n. 臨時滯留
2. stopover n. 中途停留
3. leave v. 遺忘、丟下
4. passenger n. 乘客
5. continue v. 繼續

Unit 12

兌換貨幣

精選例句

→ Where is the Currency Exchange[1]?
  貨幣兌換處在哪裡？

→ Can I exchange[2] money here?
  我可以在這裡兌換錢幣嗎？

→ Could you change this into[3] dollars?
  你可以把這個兌換為美元嗎？

→ I want to exchange some money.
  我想要兌換一些錢。

→ I want to exchange money into Taiwan dollars.
  我想要兌換成台幣。

→ I'd like to exchange some U.S. dollars to German Marks.
  我要把一些美金兌換成德國馬克。

→ Could you cash[4] a traveler's check[5]?
  你可以把旅行支票換成現金嗎？

→ Can I use U.S. dollars?
  我可以在這裡使用美金嗎？

在 機 場 **Airport**

精選句型

I want to exchange ~

我想要換~

句 型

exchange +	it
	money
	views
	my shoes
	my seats
	my order

句型範例

❖ I want to exchange my seats.
我想要換座位。

❖ I'd like to exchange some money.
我想要兌換一些錢。

Word Bank

1. Currency Exchange　n. 貨幣兌換
2. exchange　v. 兌換
3. change into　兌換為
4. cash　v. 兌換為現金
5. traveler's check　旅行支票

兌換零錢

→ How much do you want to exchange?
你想兌換多少？

→ Could you give me some small change[1] with it?
你能把這些兌換為零錢嗎？

→ Would you please break[2] this 100 U.S. dollar bill[3]?
能請您將一百元美金換成零錢嗎？

→ Can you change a dollar bill?
你可以兌換一元紙鈔嗎？

→ Can you change a dollar for ten dimes?
你能把一美元換成十個一角的銀幣嗎？

→ Could you include[4] some small change?
可以包括一些零錢嗎？

在機場  Airport

精選句型

Would you please ~?

能請您~嗎？

句型

Would you please+ 原形動詞 +

me
us
him/her
them

※及物動詞後方接受詞

句型範例

* Would you please do me a favor?
  能請你幫我忙嗎？

* Would you please call him back?
  能請你回他電話嗎？

Word Bank

1.change n. 零錢

2.break v. 兌開(大額鈔票等)

3.bill n. 鈔票

4.include v. 包括、包含

Unit
14

幣值匯率

精選例句

→ What's the exchange rate for today?
今天匯率是多少？

→ What is the exchange rate now?
現在匯率是多少？

→ How much in dollars is that?
（兌換）美元是多少？

→ I'd like to change NT$10,000 into U.S. dollars.
我要把一萬元台幣換成美金。

→ Could you tell me the procedures[1] and the exchange rate[2] for today?
你能告訴我手續和今天的匯率嗎？

→ From U.S. dollars.
從美金(換成台幣)。

→ The exchange rate from U.S. dollar to Taiwan dollar is thirty-four point five.
美金兌換成台幣的匯率是卅四點五。

精選句型

Could you tell ~?

你能告訴~嗎？

句 型

Could you tell + 受詞

※受詞：me/him/her/us/them

句 型 範 例

❖ Could you tell me the direction?
你能告訴我方向嗎？

❖ Could you tell me the solution?
你能告訴我解決的方法嗎？

Word Bank

1.procedure n. 程式、手續

2.exchange rate 匯率

Unit
15

機場常見問題

精選例句

→ Where is the person in charge?
負責的人在哪裡？

→ Will the flight be delayed?
飛機會誤點嗎？

→ Are there any other flights available?
還有其他班次可以搭乘嗎？

→ What time does the Flight 706 arrive?
706 次班機何時抵達？

→ How much is the airport tax?
機場稅是多少錢？

→ Where is the travel information counter?
旅遊服務中心在哪裡？

→ Where should I pay the airport tax?
我應該在哪裡付機場稅？

→ Is this line for non-residents?
非本國人是在這裡排隊嗎？

→ Could you page my child for me?
可以幫我廣播呼叫我的孩子嗎？

在 機 場 **Airport**

→ Do you have any maps of the downtown?
你們有市中心的地圖嗎？

→ Is there a free city map?
有沒有免費的城市地圖？

→ Where can I get to Four Season Hotel?
我要怎麼去四季飯店？

→ How much dose it cost to downtown by taxi?
坐計程車到市中心要多少錢？

→ Where should I catch a bus?
我要在哪裡搭公車？

→ Does anyone here speak Chinese?
這裡有沒有會說中文的人？

→ I don't know how to speak Japanese.
我不會說日文。

→ I come from Taiwan.
我來自台灣。

單字整理

passport 護照

visa 簽證

ticket 機票

check 檢查

check in 登記

departure 出境

arrival 入境

confirm 確認

on time 準時

delay 延誤

airport 機場

airlines 航空公司

arrival lobby 入境大廳

check-in counter 報到櫃檯

information counter 服務台

smoking room 吸菸室

ATM 自動提款機

post office 郵局

public telephone 公共電話

bank 銀行

duty-free shop 免稅商店

在機場 **Airport**

foreign currency exchange 外幣兌換

restaurant 餐廳

passenger 旅客

baggage 行李

carry-on bag 手提行李

baggage delivery 行李托運

baggage claim 提領行李

cargo terminal 貨運站

coin locker 寄物櫃

luggage scale 行李磅秤

luggage tag 行李標籤

luggage cart /trolley 手推車

boarding 登機

boarding gate 登機門

boarding pass 登機證

business class 商務艙

economy class 經濟艙

first class 頭等艙

domestic terminal 國內線航廈

flight information board 航班顯示看板

單字整理

timetable 時刻表

insurance counter 保險

international terminal 國際線航廈

transfer 轉機

transit 過境

shuttle bus 接駁車

VIP lounges 貴賓室

waiting room 候機室

greeting area 到站等候區

Chapter
2

出境
Departure

017

Unit
1

證照查驗

精選例句

→ Please take off[1] your hat and glasses.
請脫掉你的帽子和眼鏡。

→ Passport[2] and visa[3], please.
請給我護照和簽證。

→ This is my passport and visa.
這是我的護照和簽證。

→ Here you are.
給您。

→ How long are you going to stay in the USA?
您要在美國停留多久？

→ How long are you planning to stay here?
你打算在本地停留多久的時間？

→ I'll stay here for about 8 days.
我大約會在這裡停留八天。

→ I'll stay here for one more week.
我會在這裡停留一個多星期。

出境 Departure

精選句型

Please~

請~

句型

Please + 原形動詞

※此為客氣語句的祈使句型

句型範例

- ♣ Please have a seat.
  請坐！

- ♣ Please do me a favor.
  請幫我一個忙。

- ♣ Please return my call.
  請回我電話。

Word Bank

1. take off 脫去

2. passport　n. 護照

3. visa　n. 簽證

Unit
2

簽證

精選例句

→ Are you traveling alone?
你自己來旅遊的嗎？

→ I have a student visa[1].
我拿學生簽證。

→ I have a business visa[2].
我拿商務簽證。

→ I'm with my parents.
我和我父母一起來的。

→ I'm with a travel tour[3].
我是跟團的。

→ I'm alone.
我一個人（來的）。

→ I can't find my visa.
我找不到我的簽證。

出境 Departure

精選句型

Are you ~?

你~嗎？

句型

Are you + 冠詞 + 名詞 / 形容詞 / 介係詞~

句型範例

❀ Are you a student?
你是學生嗎？

❀ Are you alone?
你一個人嗎？

❀ Are you from Taiwan?
你是從台灣來的嗎？

Word Bank

1.student visa　n. 學生簽證

2.business visa　n. 商務簽證

3.travel tour 旅行團

019

Unit 3
入境原因

精選例句

→ Destination[1]?
目的地（是哪裡）？

→ What's the purpose[2] of your visit[3]?
你此行的目的是什麼？

→ It's for business[4].
我是來出差的。

→ I'm here for sightseeing[5]/touring[6].
我來這裡觀光/旅行。

→ I'm here for studies.
我來唸書的。

→ I am on vacation.
我是來渡假的。

→ I'm just passing through.
我只是路過。

→ I'm leaving for New York this afternoon.
我今天下午要去紐約。

出境 **Departure**

精選句型

What's the purpose of ~?

~的目的為何？

句 型

What is the purpose of +

| 名詞 |
| 動詞 ing |

句型範例

* What's the purpose of the instruction FCALL?
  FCALL 機構的目的為何？

* What's the purpose of making this movie?
  拍這部電影的目的為何？

Word Bank

1.destination　n. 目的地
2.purpose　n. 目的
3.visit　n. 拜訪
4.for business 出差
5.for sightseeing 觀光
6.for touring 旅遊

Unit
4

通關

精選例句

→ Why do you have them with you?
你為什麼帶這些東西？

→ Should I place my bag on the belt?
要將我的袋子放在傳送帶上嗎？

→ Where should I put my luggage?
我的行李要放哪裡？

→ Should I open my baggage?
要我打開行李嗎？

→ Just clothes[1], personal belongings[2], and some books.
只是衣物、個人用品和一些書本。

→ Those medicines[3] are prepared for myself.
這些藥物是為了我自己而準備的。

→ They are just some souvenirs[4].
它們只是一些紀念品。

→ Only personal stuff.
只有私人物品。

出境 **Departure**

精選句型

Why do you ~?

你為什麼~？

句型

Why do you + 原形動詞

句型範例

✤ Why do you want to call him?
  你為什麼想要打電話給他？

✤ Why do you own it?
  你為什麼有這個？

✤ Why do you hate Paris?
  你為什麼討厭巴黎？

Word Bank

1. clothes   n. 衣物

2. belongings   n. 攜帶物品

3. medicine   n. 藥

4. souvenir   n. 紀念品

Unit 5

申報商品

精選例句

→ Do you have any prohibited items[1]?
有沒有攜帶任何違禁品?

→ Do you have anything to declare[2]?
有沒有要申報的物品?

→ Yes, there are four bottles[3] of wine.
有的,我有四瓶酒。

→ No, I have nothing to declare.
沒有,我沒有要申報的物品。

→ No, I don't have anything to declare.
不,我沒有要申報的物品。

→ Can't I bring them in?
我不能帶他們進來?

→ You can't confiscate[4] these.
你不能沒收這些東西。

出境 Departure

精選句型

Can't I ~?

我不能~？

句型

Can't + 主詞 + 原形動詞

句型範例

✤ Can't I take pictures here?
我不能在這裡拍照嗎？

✤ Can't you listen to me?
你不能聽我說嗎？

✤ Can't you just say something?
你不能說句話嗎？

Word Bank

1.prohibited item 違禁品

2.declare v. 申報(納稅品等)

3.bottle n. 瓶子

4.confiscate v. 沒收

Unit
6

繳交稅款

精選例句

→ You have to pay tax[1] for over 50 cigarettes.
你必須要為超過的 50 支香菸付稅。

→ How much is the duty[2]?
稅金是多少？

→ How much is the duty on this?
這個要付多少稅金呢？

→ How much do I have to pay[3]?
我要付多少錢？

→ How much did you say?
你說是多少？

→ Really? I didn't know about it.
真的？我不知道這件事。

→ How should I pay for it?
我應該要如何付呢？

出境　Departure

精選句型

You have to ~

你必須要~

句型

| I/We/You/They + have He/She + has | to + 原形動詞 |

句型範例

❖ You have to be there on time.
　你必須要準時到達。

❖ She has to get back as soon as possible.
　她要盡可能回來。

Word Bank

1. tax　n. 稅

2. duty　n. 稅

3. pay　v. 支付

Unit 7

出境登機

精選例句

→ What time will boarding[1] start?
什麼時候開始登機?

→ What's the boarding time[2]?
登機時間是什麼時候?

→ Is the flight on time[3]?
班機準時起飛嗎?

→ I'm on a USA Airlines flight.
我要搭乘美國航空班機。

→ I don't know where I should board[4].
我不知道我應該在哪裡登機。

→ I think I'm at the wrong gate.
我想我走錯登機門了。

→ Where is the boarding gate?
登機門在哪裡?

→ Excuse me, where should I board?
請問,我應該到哪裡登機?

出境 Departure

精選句型

Excuse me, ~

請問，~

※打擾、請問之前的用語

句型範例

♣ Excuse me, is this 32L?
抱歉，這是 32L 嗎？

♣ Excuse me, are you Mr. Smith?
抱歉，請問你是史密斯先生嗎？

♣ Excuse me, may I say something?
抱歉，我能發言嗎？

Word Bank

1. boarding　n. 上船(或火車、飛機等)

2. boarding time　登機時間

3. on time　準時

4. board　v. 登機

MP3 024

Unit
8

尋找機位

精選例句

→ Excuse me, is this 32L?
抱歉，這是 32L 嗎？

→ I couldn't find my seat.
我找不到我的座位。

→ Would you please take me to my seat?
能請你幫我帶位嗎？

→ Could you show[1] me where my seat is?
你能告訴我我的座位在哪裡嗎？

→ Down this aisle[2], to your right/left.
順著走道，在你的右/左手邊。

→ Go straight ahead, and you will see it on
your left[3].
先直走，你就會看到在你的左手邊。

→ It's a window seat on the left[4].
是個在左邊靠窗的位子。

出境 **Departure**

精選句型

on the left/right

在左/右邊

句型

on +	the left / right your left / right your left / right hand

句型範例

❖ You'll see it on the left.
你會看見在左邊。

❖ It's on your right hand.
在你的右手邊。

Word Bank

1. show 指示

2. down this aisle 順著走道

3. on your left 在你的左手邊

4. on the left 在左手邊

Unit
9

確認機位

精選例句

→ Can I change my seat?
我能換座位嗎?

→ Can you switch[1] seats with me?
你能和我交換座位嗎?

→ Excuse me. That's my seat.
抱歉,那是我的位子。

→ I'm afraid this is my seat.
這個恐怕是我的座位。

→ I'm afraid you have my seat.
你恐怕坐了我的座位。

→ Can I move[2] to the smoking area[3]?
我能移到吸菸區嗎?

→ I'd like to move to the smoking area.
我想要換位子到吸菸區。

→ This isn't the non-smoking area[4], right?
這裡不是非吸菸區,是嗎?

出 境 **Departure**

精選句型

I'm afraid ~

恐怕~

句 型

I'm afraid + 子句 / so

句型範例

* I'm afraid you made a mistake.
  你恐怕犯錯了。

* I'm afraid it's mine.
  這恐怕是我的。

* I'm afraid so.
  恐怕是如此。

Word Bank

1.switch   v. 交換

2.move   v. 移動

3.smoking area 吸菸區

4.non-smoking area 非吸菸區

Unit 10

起飛前

精選例句

→ You can store[1] extra baggage in the overhead[2] cabinet[3].
你可以把多出來的行李放在上方的行李櫃裡。

→ Where should I put my baggage?
我應該把我的行李放哪裡？

→ I'd better fasten[4] my seatbelt[5].
我最好先繫緊我的安全帶。

→ How to fasten my seatbelt?
要怎麼繫緊安全帶？

→ I can't reach the overhead cabinet.
我搆不到上面的置物箱。

→ Be careful. It's heavy.
小心，這個很重的。

→ Would you show me how to fasten it?
你能教我怎麼繫緊嗎？

→ Can I go to the lavatory now?
我現在能去盥洗室嗎？

出境 **Departure**

精選句型

I'd better ~

我最好 ~

句 型

I'd better + 原型動詞

句型範例

❖ I'd better get off the phone.
我最好掛電話了。

❖ I'd better call him back.
我最好回他電話。

❖ I'd better finish it in 10 minutes.
我最好在十分鐘內完成。

❖ I'd better not give up.
我最好不要放棄。

Word Bank

1.store　v. 儲藏

2.overhead　a. 在頭頂上的

3.cabinet　n. 櫃子

4.fasten　v. 繫緊

5.seatbelt　n. 安全帶

Unit 11

航程

精選例句

→ How long does this flight take?
這個航程要多久的時間？

→ How long does it take to arrive?
要多久的時間才會到達？

→ Will we arrive in New York on time?
我們會準時到達紐約嗎？

→ This is a long flight[1].
這是很長的一段航程。

→ It's a long flight to the USA.
到美國是一段很長的旅程。

→ Are we passing through Japan now?
我們正穿越日本嗎？

→ How many more hours to Seattle?
到西雅圖還要幾個小時？

→ I always have jet lag[2] after a long flight.
通常在一段長程飛行後，我會有時差。

出 境 Departure

精選句型

How many ~?

還要多少～？

句型

How many + 可數名詞 + | be 動詞 / 助動詞 | +主詞

※ many 形容可數名詞 much 形容不可數名詞

句型範例

- ✤ How many hours are you taking this semester?
  這一學期你要修幾個小時？

- ✤ How many catalogues do you have?
  你有多少型錄？

Word Bank

1.long flight　n. 長時間的航程

2.jet lag 時差

Unit
12

閒聊

精選例句

➜ You look familiar[1].
你看起來很面熟。

➜ I'm David. You are?
我是大衛。您的（大名）是？

➜ Joan. Nice to meet[2] you, David.
(我是)瓊。很高興認識你，大衛。

➜ Nice to meet you, too.
(我)也很高興認識你。

➜ Where are you from?
您從哪裡來的？

➜ I'm here from London to see my friends.
我來自倫敦，是為了探望朋友。

➜ It is nice talking to you.
很高興和你聊天。

➜ Nice talking to you, too.
我也很高興和你聊天。

出境 Departure

精選句型

Nice talking to you.
很高興和你聊天。

句型

Nice + 動詞 ing

※完整句型為 It's nice~

句型範例

- ♣ Nice meeting you.
  很高興和你見面。

- ♣ Nice having a talk with you.
  很高興和你聊天。

- ♣ Nice seeing you again.
  很高興又看見你。

Word Bank

1. familiar   a. 熟悉的

2. meet   v. 遇見

Unit
13

餐飲

精選例句

➤ What time will we have a meal[1] served?
我們幾點用餐？

➤ What do you have?
你們有什麼（餐點）？

➤ I'd like beef, please.
我要吃牛肉，謝謝。

➤ Noodles, please.
我要（選）麵。

➤ Do you have a vegetarian meal[2]?
你們有素食餐點嗎？

➤ Coffee, please.
請給我咖啡。

➤ May I have some more tea, please?
我能再多要點茶嗎？

出境 Departure

精選句型

What time ~?

什麼時間~？

句 型

What time + | 助動詞 / be 動詞 | + 主詞

句型範例

❧ What time will you arrive in Paris?
你什麼時間會抵達巴黎？

❧ What time did you get there?
你什麼時間到那裡的？

❧ What time are you going?
你什麼時間要去？

Word Bank

1.meal n. 餐點

2.vegetarian meal 素食餐點

MP3 030

Unit 14

請求提供餐飲

精選例句

➜ I'm still hungry[1].
我還是很餓。

➜ Do you have instant noodles[2]?
你們有泡麵嗎？

➜ May I have a glass of orange juice[3]?
我能要一杯柳橙汁嗎？

➜ May I have something to drink?
我能喝點飲料嗎？

➜ I'm a little thirsty[4].
我有一點口渴。

➜ Do you have any cold drinks[5]?
你們有任何冷飲嗎？

➜ By the way, could you get me some beer[6] too?
你能順便給我一些啤酒嗎？

➜ May I have a glass of hot water? Not too hot, please.
我可以要一杯熱開水嗎？不要太熱。

出境  Departure

精選句型

May I ~?

我能~嗎？

句型

May I + 原形動詞

句型範例

- ♣ May I help you?
  需要我協助嗎？

- ♣ May I have your name, please?
  請問您的大名？

- ♣ May I have some more tea, please?
  我能再多要點茶嗎？

Word Bank

1.hungry a. 飢餓的
2.instant noodles 泡麵
3.orange juice 柳橙汁
4.thirsty a. 口乾的
5.cold drinks 冷飲
6.beer n. 啤酒

🎵 031

Unit
15

不舒服

✈ I don't feel well.
我覺得不舒服。

✈ I feel airsick[1].
我覺得暈機。

✈ I have a headache[2].
我頭痛。

✈ I have a pain[3] here.
我這裡痛。

✈ I have a stomachache[4].
我胃痛。

✈ I have a fever[5].
我發燒了。

✈ I need a doctor.
我需要醫生。

✈ Do you have airsickness bags?
你有嘔吐袋嗎？

出境 Departure

精選句型

I feel airsick.

我感覺暈機。

句型

I feel + 形容詞

句型範例

* I feel sick.
  我感覺生病了。

* I feel terrible.
  我感覺很糟糕。

* I feel so bad.
  我感覺很差。

* I feel painful.
  我感覺很痛。

Word Bank

1. airsick a. 暈機的
2. headache n. 頭痛
3. pain n. 疼痛
4. stomachache n. 胃痛
5. fever n. 發燒

MP3 032

Unit 16

填寫表格

精選例句

→ Will you give me a customs declaration[1]?
能給我一張海關申報單嗎？

→ May I have another embarkation card[2]?
我可以再要一張旅客入境記錄卡嗎？

→ Could you tell me how to fill it in[3]?
你能告訴我怎麼填寫嗎？

→ How should I fill this in?
我要怎麼填寫這張表格？

→ Could you show me what to write here?
你能告訴我這裡要填什麼嗎？

→ Fill in this blank[4] with my address?
在這個表格填寫我的地址嗎？

→ I need that, too.
我也需要那個。

出境 **Departure**

精選句型

May I have ~?

我能~嗎？

句 型

May I have + 名詞

句型範例

* ✤ May I have your name?
  請問您的大名？

* ✤ May I have a glass of water?
  我能要一杯水喝嗎？

* ✤ May I have an invitation, please?
  我能要一張邀請函嗎？

Word Bank

1.customs declaration　n. 海關申報

2.embarkation card　入境記錄卡

3.fill in　填寫

4.blank　n. 空格

Unit
17

請求協助

精選例句

→ Would you do me a favor[1]?
你能幫我一個忙嗎？

→ Would you put this in the overhead cabinet?
您可以幫我把它放進上方的櫃子裡嗎？

→ Do you have a Chinese newspaper?
你們有中文報紙嗎？

→ I feel cold. May I have a blanket[2]?
我覺得有一些冷，我能要一條毯子嗎？

→ May I have an earphone[3], please?
可以給我一副耳機嗎？

→ Any Chinese speakers?
有沒有會說中文的人？

→ What is the local time[4] in Seattle?
西雅圖當地時間是幾點鐘？

→ What is the temperature[5] in the USA?
美國現在溫度多少？

出境 **Departure**

(精選句型)

do me a favor
幫我一個忙

句 型

do + | me
us/them
him/her | a favor

句型範例

❖ Would you please do me a favor?
　能請你幫我一個忙嗎？

❖ Please do me a favor.
　請你幫我一個忙。

❖ Do me a favor, please?
　幫我一個忙好嗎？

Word Bank

1. do sb. a favor 幫某人一個忙
2. blanket　n. 毯子
3. earphone　n. 耳機
4. local time 當地時間
5. temperature　n. 溫度

MP3 034

Unit 18

使用設備

精選例句

➤ How should I turn this light on[1]?
我要怎麼打開這燈？

➤ How should I operate[2] this?
這個我要怎麼操作？

➤ Where is the lavatory[3]?
盥洗室在哪裡？

➤ Is this vacant[4]?
(廁所)是空的嗎？

➤ The lavatory is occupied[5].
廁所裡面有人。

➤ It doesn't work.
這個不能運轉。

➤ Can I recline[6] my seat back now?
我現在可以將椅背往後靠嗎？

出境 Departure

精選句型

How should I~?

我要如何~?

句型

How should I + 原形動詞

句型範例

❖ How should I spell this vocabulary?
我要如何拼這個單字?

❖ How should I exchange it?
我要如何更換?

❖ How should I operate this machine?
我要如何操作這個機器?

Word Bank

1.turn on 打開
2.operate v. 操作
3.lavatory n. 廁所
4.vacant a. 未被佔用的
5.occupied a. 在使用的
6.recline v. (座椅)靠背可活動後仰

Unit 19
回應他人的協助

精選例句

✈ Sorry to bother[1] you.
很抱歉麻煩您了。

✈ Yes, please.
是的(我需要)，麻煩你了。

✈ No, thank you.
不用，謝謝！

✈ I can arrange[2] it by myself[3]. Thank you.
我可以自己來。謝謝你。

✈ Thank you for your help.
感謝你的協助。

✈ Thank you so much.
非常感謝。

出境 **Departure**

精選句型

Thank you for ~

感謝你的 ~

句 型

Thank you for your + 名詞

句型範例

* Thank you for your support.
  感謝你的支持。
* Thank you for your patience.
  感謝你的耐心。
* Thank you for your donation.
  感謝你的贊助。

Word Bank

1.bother v. 煩擾、打擾

2.arrange v. 安排

3.by myself 靠自己

Unit 20

請鄰座協助

精選例句

→ Excuse me.
借過。

→ Sorry to bother[1] you.
抱歉打擾你。

→ Would you please turn down[2] your voice?
你可以小聲一點嗎？

→ I need to get some sleep.
我需要睡一下。

→ Can you hold[3] this for me?
可以幫我拿一下嗎？

→ Thank you for your help.
謝謝你的幫助。

→ Do you mind?
你介意嗎？

出境 Departure

精選句型

I need to get some sleep.
我需要睡一下。

句型

get + 睡眠、休息
交通工具
疾病

句型範例

❧ You'd better get some rest.
你最好休息一下。

❧ Everyone in our room got flu.
我們房間裡的所有人都患了流行性感冒。

❧ We must get the ten o'clock plane.
我們一定要趕上十點的飛機。

Word Bank

1.bother v. 打擾

2.turn down 壓低（聲量）

3.hold v. 拿

Unit
21

短暫交談後

精選例句

→ It's a pleasure to meet you.
很高興認識你。

→ Nice talking to you.
很高興和你聊天。

→ Have[1] a safe[2] trip[3].
祝你旅途平安。

→ Safe flight.
旅途平安!

→ Have a good flight back[4].
祝你回程旅途平安。

→ Good luck.
祝你好運。

→ Take care.
保重。

→ Bye.
再見!

出境 **Departure**

精選句型

Have a safe trip.

祝你旅途平安。

句 型

Have + 祝福語句

句型範例

❖ Have a safe trip to California.
  祝你一路平安到加州。

❖ Have a good night.
  祝你好眠。

❖ Have fun.
  好好玩。

Word Bank

1.have v. 祝福

2.safe a. 平安的

3.trip n. 旅程

4.back adv. 回來的

單字整理

destination 目的地

pass through 過境

student visa 學生簽證

business visa 商務簽證

sightseeing visa 觀光簽證

travel tour 旅行團

prohibited items 違禁品

declare 申報

pay 支付

tax 稅務

cash 現金

coin 硬幣

exchange 兌換

airport tax 機場稅

captain 機長

flight attendant 空服員(不分性別)

seat 座位

aisle seat 走道座位

window seat 靠窗座位

smoking area 吸菸區

non-smoking area 非吸菸區

出境 Departure

head sets 耳機

airsick 暈機的

headache 頭痛

pain 疼痛

stomachache 胃痛

fever 發燒

thirsty 口渴的

blanket 毯子

pillow 枕頭

aspirin 阿司匹靈

meal 餐點

drink 飲料

movie 電影

occupied 使用中(廁所)

vacant 無人使用(廁所)

overhead cabinet 上方櫃子

fasten 繫緊

seatbelt 安全帶

life vest 救生衣

oxygen mask 氧氣面罩

單字整理

fasten seat belt 扣緊安全帶

airsickness bag 嘔吐袋

turbulence 亂流

temperature 氣溫

local time 當地時間

jet lag 時差

customs declaration 海關申報單

embarkation card 入境記錄卡

fill in 填寫

投宿旅館
Hotel

039

詢問空房

精選例句

→ Do you have any rooms available[1]?
你們還有空房間嗎？

→ Do you still have a vacancy[2]?
你們還有空房嗎？

→ Do you have any double rooms available for tonight?
你們今晚有雙人房的空房嗎？

→ Do you have any vacancies for tonight?
你們今晚有空房嗎？

→ Do you have a single room[3] for 2 nights?
你們有兩晚的單人空房嗎？

→ I plan to stay here for 4 nights.
我計劃要在這裡住四晚。

→ I'd like a room for two with separate[4] beds.
我要一間有兩張床的房間。

投宿旅館 **Hotel**

精選句型

Do you have any ~?
你們有任何~嗎？

句型

have any +	可數名詞複數
	不可數名詞單數

句型範例

* Do you have any ideas?
  你有任何想法嗎？

* Do you have any baggage?
  你有任何行李嗎？

Word Bank

1. available a. 空房的

2. vacancy n. 空房

3. single room 單人房間

4. separate a. 分開的

Unit
2
詢問房價

精選例句

→ How much per night?
(住宿)一晚要多少錢？

→ How much will it be?
要多少錢？

→ How much should I pay for a week?
一個星期得付多少錢？

→ Do you have any cheaper[1] rooms?
你們有便宜一點的房間嗎？

→ Do you have any less expensive rooms?
你們有沒有不貴的房間？

→ How much for a single room[2]?
單人房多少錢？

→ Are meals included[3]?
有包括餐點嗎？

→ Does the room rate[4] include breakfast?
住宿費有包括早餐嗎？

投宿旅館 **Hotel**

(精選句型)

How much per night?

每一晚要多少錢?

句型

per + 名詞

句型範例

❖ The lunch is \$50 per person.
午餐是每人五十元。

❖ You have to take one tablet per day.
你每一天要吃一錠。

Word Bank

1.cheaper a. 較便宜的

2.single room 單人房

3.included a. 被包括的

4.room rate 房價

MP3 041

Unit 3

訂房

精選例句

→ OK. I'll take it.
好，我要住房。

→ I'd like a room for one.
我要一間單人房。

→ Do you have a twin room[1]?
你們有兩張單人床的房間嗎？

→ I need three single rooms for tonight.
我今晚需要三間單人房間。

→ I want a room with a sauna[2].
我想要一間有蒸汽浴的房間。

→ I want a room with good view[3].
我想要一間有好景觀的房間。

→ I'd like a room with a king size bed[4].
我要一間有兩張床的房間。

投宿旅館 **Hotel**

精選句型

I'll take it.

我要住房。

※本句也可以譯為「我決定要買這個」。

句 型

S + will + 原型動詞

句型範例

✤ I'll try to contact him.
我會試著聯絡他。

✤ Matthew will figure it out.
馬修會想出辦法。

Word Bank

1.twin room 雙人房

2.sauna n. 蒸汽

3.view n. 景觀

4.king size bed 加大床

042

預約／取消預約

精選例句

→ No, I didn't have a reservation[1].
沒有,我沒有預約。

→ I made a reservation.
我有預約。

→ I made a reservation for 1 single room.
我有預約一間單人房。

→ My company booked a single room for me.
我的公司有幫我訂了一間單人房。

→ We made a reservation last week.
我們上個星期有預約。

→ I'd like to book a room for my boss.
我要幫我的老闆預約一個房間。

→ I'd like to cancel[2] my reservation.
我要取消我的預約。

→ Can you check[3] my reservation?
你可以查一下我的預約嗎?

100

投宿旅館 (Hotel)

精選句型

I made a reservation.

我有預約。

句型範例

A：How can I help you?
需要我幫忙嗎?

B：I made a reservation.
我有預約。

A：OK. May I have your name, please?
好的,請給我您的大名。

B：Sure. My name is David Wang.
好。我是王大衛。

Word Bank

1. reservation　n. 預約

2. cancel　v. 取消

3. check　v. 確認

Unit 5
臨時訂不到房間

精選例句

→ I'm sorry, sir, but our room are fully booked[1].
抱歉，先生，我們全部客滿了。

→ Where are we going to find a room at this time?
這時候我們要去哪裡找房間？

→ Could you recommend[2] another hotel?
你可以推薦另一個飯店嗎？

→ Would you put me on your waiting list[3]?
你可以幫我排進候補名單上嗎？

→ Where can I find a hotel nearby[4]?
這附近哪裡有旅館？

→ Do you know any motels around here?
你知道這附近有沒有汽車旅館？

投宿旅館 **Hotel**

精選句型

Where can I find ~?

哪裡能找到~？

句型

Where can someone + 原形動詞

句型範例

❖ Where can we reach him?
  我們可以在哪裡聯絡上他？

❖ Where can I get a job?
  我能到哪裡找到工作？

❖ Where can he go?
  他能去哪裡？

Word Bank

1.book   v. 預訂

2.recommend   v. 推薦

3.waiting list 候補名單

4.nearby   adv. 在附近

MP3 044

Unit 6

登記住宿

精選例句

→ Did you make a reservation?
您有預約（住宿）嗎？

→ I'd like to check in[1].
我要登記住宿。

→ I have a reservation. My name is Tom Jones.
我有預約訂房。我的名字是湯姆・瓊斯。

→ Can I check in now?
我現在可以登記住宿嗎？

→ When can I check in?
我什麼時候可以登記住宿？

→ I have a reservation for 2 nights.
我已訂了兩天住宿。

→ Here is the confirmation slip[2].
這是確認單。

→ I'd like to stay for 2 more nights.
我想再多住兩晚。

精選句型

Here is the confirmation slip.

這是確認單。

句型

here is + 名詞

句型範例

* Here is our latest price sheet.
  這是我們最新的報價單。
* Here is a detailed list of our offer.
  這是我們的一份報價清單。

Word Bank

1. check in　n. 登記住宿
2. confirmation slip 確認單

MP3 045

Unit
7
飯店用餐

精選例句

➜ I forgot to bring my coupon[1] with me.
我忘了帶我的餐券。

➜ Can I make a reservation for dinner?
我可以預約晚餐訂位嗎?

➜ What time is breakfast/lunch/dinner served?
早餐/午餐/晚餐什麼時候供應?

➜ What time is the restaurant open until?
餐廳供餐到什麼時候?

➜ Where is breakfast served?
早餐在哪裡供應?

➜ I want to reserve a table[2] for dinner tonight.
我想預訂一桌今天的晚餐。

➜ I'd like a table by the window.
我要靠窗戶的座位。

➜ Please charge[3] it to my room. It's Room 714.
請將帳算在我的房間費用上,房間號碼是七一四。

投宿旅館 **Hotel**

精選句型

I forgot ~

我忘了 ~

句 型

forget +
to do something
名詞

句型範例

✤ I forgot to call him.
我忘了打電話給他。

✤ Did you forget the exam?
你忘了考試這件事？

Word Bank

1. coupon   n. 配給券

2. reserve a table   預定座位

3. charge   v. 要價

MP3 046

Unit 8
表明身分

精選例句

➜ I'm Jack Smith of Room 320.
我是320號房的傑克‧史密斯。

➜ My name is Jack Smith.
我的名字是傑克‧史密斯。

➜ This is Room 613.
這是613號房。

➜ My room number[1] is 1201.
我的房間號碼是1201。

➜ Room 756. Key, please.
房號756。請給我鑰匙。

➜ I am in room 711.
我在711號房間。

投宿旅館 **Hotel** ✈

精選句型

My name is Jack.

我的名字是傑克。

句 型

| My name is
I am
This is | + 名字 |

句型範例

A：Hello?
　　哈囉？

B：Hi. This is Peter Chang.
　　嗨！我是彼得張。

A：Hi, Peter. What's up?
　　嗨，彼得。有什麼事嗎？

B：Do you have any plans tonight?
　　你今晚有事嗎？

Word Bank

1.room number 房號

MP3 047

Unit 9
客房服務

精選例句

→ Can I order room service now?
我現在可以叫客房服務嗎?

→ Do you offer room service?
你們有提供客房服務嗎?

→ What do you have?
你們有什麼?

→ Would you bring us a bottle of [1] champagne[2]?
你能帶一瓶香檳給我們嗎?

→ I'd like four sandwiches.
我要點四份三明治。

→ Let's see, and I want a chicken sandwich.
我想想,還有我要一份雞肉三明治。

→ Is there a service charged[3]?
要加服務費嗎?

→ Please add[4] the cost[5] to my room bill[6].
請把這個費用加到我房間的帳單上。

投宿旅館　**Hotel**

(精選句型)

What do you have?

你們有什麼？

| 句　型 |

What + | do+ you/they / does + he/she | +原形動詞

句型範例

❖ What do you want?
你想要什麼？

❖ What do they plan to do?
他們計劃做什麼？

❖ What does he try to do?
他想做什麼？

Word Bank

1.a bottle of~ 一瓶~
2.champagne n. 香檳
3.charge v. 收費
4.add v. 加入
5.cost n. 費用
6.room bill 房間的帳單

MP3 048

Unit 10
衣物送洗

→ Do you have laundry service[1]?
你們有洗衣服務嗎?

→ I have some laundry[2].
我有一些衣服要送洗。

→ I'd like to send my suit to the cleaners[3].
我要把我的西裝送洗。

→ When can I have them returned?
我什麼時候可以把它們拿回來?

→ I haven't gotten the coat back that I sent to the cleaners yesterday.
我昨天送洗的外套還沒送回來。

→ From what time do you accept[4] the laundry?
你們從什麼時候起受理送洗的衣物?

→ Should I put it in the plastic bag and leave it on the bed?
我應該把它放在塑膠袋裡,然後放在床上嗎?

投宿旅館 **Hotel**

精選句型

When can I ~ ?

我什麼時候可以~？

句 型

When can +
| I |
| you |
| they/we |
| he/she |
| 人名 |
+ 原形動詞

句型範例

✤ When can we meet him?
我們什麼時候可以見他？

✤ When can David finish it?
大衛什麼時候可以完成？

Word Bank

1. laundry service 洗衣服務

2. laundry　n. 送洗的衣服

3. cleaners　n. 乾洗店

4. accept　v. 接受、領受

Unit 11

設施故障

精選例句

✈ There is no hot water.
沒有熱水。

✈ The dryer doesn't work.
吹風機壞了。

✈ Something wrong with the toilet.
廁所有點問題。

✈ The lock of my room is broken.
我房間的鎖壞了。

✈ The toilet doesn't work properly[1].
廁所壞了。

✈ The filament has broken.
燈絲壞了。

✈ The water doesn't drain[2].
水流不出來。

✈ My phone is out of order[3].
我的電話故障。

投宿旅館　Hotel

精選句型

The lock is broken.

鎖壞了。

句型

be + 動詞過去分詞

句型範例

✤ The work was done.
工作完成。

✤ The door was shut.
門關起來。

✤ They were finished.
他們完成了。

Word Bank

1.properly　adv. 正確地

2.drain　v. 使流出

3.out of order 故障

Unit
12

與櫃臺溝通

精選例句

→ Where can I find the tourist information counter[1]?
   請問旅客服務台在哪裡？

→ Where is the locker[2]?
   寄物櫃在哪裡？

→ Do I have any messages[3]?
   我有任何的留言嗎？

→ Where can I buy souvenirs[4] nearby?
   這附近有哪裡我可以買紀念品的？

→ How should I get there?
   我要怎麼到那裡？

→ Can I get there on foot[5]?
   用走的可以到嗎？

→ What tourist attractions would you recommend?
   有什麼觀光名勝可以推薦給我的嗎？

投宿旅館 **Hotel**

精選句型

Where can I find ~?

請問~在哪裡？

句 型

Where can I find + 尋找的人/事/物

句型範例

✤ Where can I find David?
我可以在哪裡找到大衛？

✤ Where can I find this book?
我可以在哪裡找到這本書？

Word Bank

1. tourist information counter
   旅客服務台
2. locker n. 衣物櫃
3. message n. 口信、信息
4. souvenir n. 紀念品
5. on foot 步行

Unit 13

房間鑰匙

精選例句

✈ Do I have to leave the room key when I go out[1]?
在我外出時必須要留下房間鑰匙嗎？

✈ I have lost my room key.
我遺失了我的房間鑰匙了。

✈ I left[2] my key in my room.
我把鑰匙放在房間裡（忘了帶出來）。

✈ I locked myself out[3].
我把自己反鎖在外面。

✈ Key to Room 306, please.
我要拿房號306的鑰匙。

✈ My room number is 306.
我的房間號碼是306。

投宿旅館 **Hotel**

精選句型

I locked myself out.
我把自己反鎖在外面。

句型

lock+ | myself/ourselves
yourself/yourselves
themselves
himself/herself | + out

句型範例

❖ I locked myself out of my room.
我把自己關在房間外了。

❖ I locked myself out of my car.
我把自己反鎖在車外了。

Word Bank

1. go out 外出

2. left v. 遺留
（leave 的過去式）

3. lock myself out 將自己反鎖

052

Unit
14

要求提供服務

✈ Give me a wake-up call[1] at ten, please.
請在十點打電話叫醒我。

✈ I'd like an extra pillow[2] for Room 316.
我要在316房多加一個枕頭。

✈ I'd like a wake-up call every morning.
我每一天都要早上叫醒(的服務)。

✈ I can't find any towels in my room.
我的房裡沒有毛巾。

✈ Could you bring some towels right now[3]?
請你馬上送幾條毛巾過來好嗎？

✈ Could you keep my baggage till two o'clock?
請你幫我保管行李到兩點鐘好嗎？

✈ I'd like to pick up my baggage.
我要拿行李。

投宿旅館 **Hotel**

精選句型

Give me a wake-up call .

打電話叫醒我。

句型

Give + me/us / you / them / him/her + 名詞

※祈使句用法

句型範例

✤ Give me a break.
饒了我吧！

✤ Give him a chance.
給他一個機會。

Word Bank

1. wake-up call 早晨叫醒服務

2. pillow n. 枕頭

3. right now 馬上

MP3 053

Unit
15
退房

精選例句

→ When is check-out time[1]?
退房的時間是什麼時候？

→ When should I check out[2]?
我應該什麼時候退房？

→ Check out, please.
請結帳。

→ I'd like to check out.
我要結帳。

→ Here is the room key.
這是房間鑰匙。

→ I'd like to check out. My bill, please.
我要退房。請給我帳單。

→ I'm ready to leave.
我要走了。

→ Please have someone bring my baggage down.
請派人把我的行李拿下來。

投宿旅館 （Hotel）

精選句型

Have someone ~

派人 ~

句型

have someone + 原形動詞

句型範例

* Have someone help you.
  派人來幫你。

* Have someone call him.
  派人來打電話給他。

* Have someone look into this for me.
  派人替我查一查。

1
2
3

Word Bank

1. check-out time 退房的時間

2. check out 退房

MP3 054

Unit 16

結帳

精選例句

→ How much does it charge?
這要收多少錢？

→ Put it on my hotel bill[1], please.
請算在我的住宿費裡。

→ Can I pay with a traveler's check?
我可以付旅行支票嗎？

→ Do you take credit cards[2]?
你們收信用卡嗎？

→ I'll pay by cash[3].
我會付現金。

→ There is something wrong with the bill.
帳單恐怕有點問題。

→ Are the service charges and tax included?
是否包括服務費和稅金嗎？

→ Are there any additional[4] charges?
是否有其他附加費用？

投宿旅館 **Hotel**

精選句型

How much does it charge?

這要收多少錢？

句型

how much + 助動詞 + 主詞 +
| cost |
| spend |
| say |
| ask |

句型範例

✤ How much does it cost?
這要收多少錢？

✤ How much does it spend?
這要花費多少錢？

Word Bank

1. bill　n. 帳單

2. credit card　n. 信用卡

3. cash　n. 現金、現款

4. additional　a. 附加的、額外的

Unit 17

飯店常用語

→ Who is it, please?
是誰？

→ I'd like to change my room.
我想換房間。

→ If someone comes to see me, please give him this message.
如果有人來找我，請將這留言交給他。

→ Is there a beauty salon in the hotel?
旅館中有美容院嗎？

→ Could you call me a taxi, please? I'm going to the airport.
請你幫我叫部計程車好嗎？我要去機場。

→ Is this coin[1] all right for telephones?
這個硬幣可以打電話嗎？

→ Could you connect[2] me with the telephone directory assistance[3]?
可以幫我接查號台嗎？

→ How should I call a number outside this hotel?
我要怎麼從飯店撥外線出去？

投宿旅館　(**Hotel**)

精選句型

Call me a taxi, please.

請幫我叫一部計程車。

句 型

call someone + 冠詞+名詞
　　　　　　　 名字/身份

句型範例

❖ Call me a taxi.
幫我叫一部計程車。

❖ Just call me Jack.
叫我傑克。

❖ Call me a genius!
稱呼我是天才吧！

Word Bank

1.coin　n. 硬幣

2.connect　v. 給...接通電話

3.telephone directory assistance
查號台

Unit 18

保管物品

精選例句

→ May I leave[1] my baggage with you?
我可以把行李留在你這裡嗎？

→ Could you take care of[2] my baggage?
你可以幫我保管我的行李嗎？

→ Please look after[3] my baggage.
請保管我的行李。

→ Where can I put my baggage?
我可以把我的行李放在哪裡？

→ Could you look after my baggage for an hour?
可以幫我保管行李一小時嗎？

→ Will you keep these valuables[4] for me?
請幫我保管這些貴重物品好嗎？

→ I'll take them before 5 o'clock this afternoon.
我今天下午五點前會來拿。

投宿旅館　**Hotel**

精選句型

take care of my baggage
保管我的行李

句型

take care of + | someone / something |

句型範例

❖ Take care of yourself.
好好照顧你自己。

❖ I have to take care of my baby.
我要照顧我的孩子。

❖ Could you take care of my business?
可以幫我料理我的事業嗎?

Word Bank

1.leave v. 放置

2.take care of 照顧

3.look after 照料

4.valuable n. 貴重物品

057

精選例句

✈ Is there anyone here who speaks Chinese?
這裡有誰會說中文嗎?

✈ Are there any spots[1] around here?
這附近有沒有旅遊勝地?

✈ May I have a map of the city?
請問有這個城市的地圖嗎?

✈ Where does the bus tour go?
這個公車旅行團要去哪裡?

✈ I'd like to make a reservation of the city tour.
我要預約參加市區旅遊。

✈ Would you please take a picture[2] for me?
可以請你幫我拍照嗎?

✈ I want to have this film[3] developed[4].
我想要去沖洗相片。

投宿旅館 **Hotel**

精選句型

take a picture for me

幫我拍照

句型

do something for someone

句型範例

* I can paint the fence for you.
  我可以幫你漆圍牆。

* Would you wrap it for me?
  你可以幫我包裝嗎？

* Will you send this letter for me?
  你可以幫我寄這封信嗎？

1 3 1

Word Bank

1.spot n .旅遊勝地

2.take a picture 照相

3.film n. 相片

4.develop v. 沖洗相片

Unit 20

一般諮詢

精選例句

✈ Who is in charge[1]?
負責的人是誰？

✈ Do you know where the nearest[2] hospital is?
你知道最近的醫院在哪裡嗎？

✈ Where can I get some pain-killers[3]?
我要到哪裡拿止痛劑？

✈ Where is the nearest cyber café?
最近的網咖在哪裡？

✈ Where is the shopping mall[4] in the city?
這個城市的購物中心在哪裡呢？

✈ Can I make a long distance call[5] here?
我可以在這裡打長途電話嗎？

✈ Where can I exchange money?
我可以在哪裡兌換錢幣？

投宿旅館 （ Hotel

精選句型

I want to speak to the person in charge.

我要和負責的人說話。

句 型

someone + be 動詞 + in charge + (of~)

句型範例

❖ I'm in charge of this bar.
我負責這間酒吧。

❖ Who is in charge here?
這裡誰負責？

Word Bank

1. charge n. 負責
2. nearest a. 最近的
3. pain-killer n. 止痛劑
4. shopping mall 購物中心
5. long distance call 長途電話

精選例句

✈ I'll stay here for another[1] 5 nights.
我還要另外再住五天。

✈ I'll stay here for another two weeks.
我還要另外再住兩個星期。

✈ My flight doesn't leave[2] until late this afternoon.
我的班機下午才會飛。

✈ Is there any possibility of an extended[3] check-out time?
有沒有可能可以延遲結帳呢？

✈ I don't want to cause[4] any problems.
我不想造成麻煩。

✈ I'll understand if you can't do it.
如果不可以的話，我可以理解。

投宿旅館 **Hotel**

精選句型

I don't want to cause any problems.

我不想造成麻煩。

句 型

cause +
| (someone) + something |
| someone + to +原形動詞 |

句型範例

✤ What caused him to quit his job?
是什麼原因使他辭職的?

✤ I'm afraid I'm causing you much trouble.
我怕給你增添很多麻煩。

Word Bank

1.another a. 另外的

2.leave v. 離開

3.extended a. 延伸的

4.cause v. 造成

單字整理

 06

check in 登記住宿

check out 退房

vacancy 空房

available 空房的

confirmation slip 確認單

counter 櫃臺

operator 總機

receptionist 接待員

separate 分開的

single room 單人房

double room 雙人房

twin beds room 兩張單人床的雙人房

room rate 房價

sauna 蒸氣

view 景觀

reservation 預約

cancel 取消

check 確認

book 預訂

coupon 配給券

room number 房號

投宿旅館 **Hotel**

key 鑰匙

floor 樓層

elevator 電梯

lobby 大廳

restaurant 餐廳

bar 酒吧

map 地圖

store 商店

laundry service 洗衣服務

laundry 送洗的衣服

cleaners 乾洗店

locker 衣物櫃

message 信息

souvenir 紀念品

on foot 步行

tourist attractions 觀光名勝

room service 房間服務

wake-up call 早晨叫醒服務

tip 小費

pillow 枕頭

單字整理

valuable 貴重物品

baggage 行李

charge 收費

cost 費用

bill 帳單

credit card 信用卡

cash 現金

traveler's check 旅行支票

receipt 收據

Chapter

4

電話聯絡
Phone

Unit 1

去電找人

精選例句

✈ Is David around[1]?
大衛在嗎?

✈ Is Annie in today?
安妮今天在嗎?

✈ Is Brian in the office now?
布萊恩現在在辦公室嗎裡?

✈ May I speak to Dr. Brown?
我能和布朗教授說話嗎?

✈ May I speak to David, please?
我能和大衛說話嗎?

✈ Could I talk to Carrie or Sunny?
我能和凱莉或桑尼說話嗎?

✈ This is David calling for[2] Miss Jones.
我是大衛打電話來要找瓊斯小姐。

✈ Is this Mrs. Jones?
您是瓊斯太太嗎?

精選句型

May I speak to ~?

我能和~説話嗎？

句 型

May I + | speak / talk | + to + 人名

句型範例

✤ May I speak to David, please?
我能和大衛説話嗎？

✤ May I talk to Peter?
我能和彼得説話嗎？

Word Bank

1.around　adv. 附近

2.call for　來電找（某人）

MP3 062

Unit 2
表明身分

 精選例句

→ This is David Lee calling.
我是李大衛打電話。

→ Hello, this is David Lee calling from Taiwan.
哈囉！我是從台灣打電話來的李大衛。

→ This is David calling from Tech Company.
我是科技公司的大衛打電話來。

→ Could you put me through[1] to Peter? This is David.
可以幫我將電話轉給彼得嗎？我是大衛。

→ Hi, John. This is David.
嗨，約翰，我是大衛。

→ EZ Tech Company. Good morning.
早安，這是 EZ 高科技公司。

電話聯絡　**Phone**

精選句型

This is David calling.

這是大衛打來的電話。

句 型

This is + 人名 + | calling |
| speaking |

句型範例

✤ This is David calling from Taiwan.
這是大衛從台灣打電話來。

✤ This is Peter speaking.
我是彼得。

Word Bank

1.put me through 把我的電話轉接

Unit 3
詢問受話方現況

精選例句

→ Is David off the line?
大衛講完電話了嗎?

→ Where is he?
他人在哪裡?

→ May I have his phone number?
可以給我他的電話號碼嗎?

→ When will he come back?
他什麼時候回來?

→ Do you know when he will be back?
你知道他什麼時候會回來?

→ Do you know where I can reach[1] him?
你知道我在哪裡可以聯絡上他嗎?

→ Do you have any idea[2] where he is?
你知道他在哪裡嗎?

電話聯絡 **Phone**

精選句型

Do you know ~?

你知道 ~ ？

句 型

Do you know +
| what |
| when |
| where |
| who |
| which |
| how |
+ 主詞 + 動詞

句型範例

✤ Do you know where she is?
你知道她在哪裡？

✤ Do you know when he'll be there?
你知道他什麼時候會在那裡？

✤ Do you know which one is better?
你知道哪一個比較好？

Word Bank

1.reach sb. 聯絡某人

2.have any idea 是否知道

Unit
4
回電

精選例句

→ I'm returning your call[1].
我現在回你電話。

→ You called me last night, didn't you?
你昨天打電話給我，不是嗎？

→ Thank you for returning my call.
謝謝你回我電話。

→ That's all right. I'll try to call him later.
沒關係。我晚一點再打電話給他。

→ I'll try again later.
我晚一點再試一次（打電話）。

→ When should I call back[2] then?
那我應該什麼時候回電？

→ Can I call again in 10 minutes?
我可以十分鐘後再打電話過來嗎？

→ Would you tell him I called?
你能告訴他我來電過嗎？

電話聯絡 Phone

精選句型

You called me, didn't you?
你打電話給我，不是嗎？

句 型

主詞+

| 一般動詞（現在式）~, + don't |
| 一般動詞（過去式）~, + didn't |

+主詞?

句型範例

❖ You try to make her happy, don't you?
你試著要讓她快樂，不是嗎？

❖ You went to the library, didn't you?
你有去了圖書館，不是嗎？

Word Bank

1.return sb's call 回某人電話

2.call back 回電

Unit 5
本人接電話

精選例句

→ Speaking.
請說。

→ This is Kate Simon.
我是凱特．賽門。

→ This is he/she.
我就是你要找的人。

→ It's me.
我就是。

→ I can't talk to you now.
我現在不能講（電話）。

→ I'm really busy now. I'll call you later.
我現在真的很忙。我待會打電話給你。

→ Who is calling, please?
您是哪一位？

→ Would you mind¹ calling back² later?
你介意等一下再打電話過來嗎？

電話聯絡 **Phone**

精選句型

Would you mind calling back?

你介意再打電話過來嗎?

句型

mind + 動詞 ing / someone's + 名詞 / if 子句

句型範例

❖ Do you mind telling us more about you?
你介意再多告訴我們一些你的事嗎?

❖ Do you mind my smoking?
你介意我抽煙嗎?

❖ Do you mind if I sit down?
你介意我坐下嗎?

Word Bank

1. mind　v. 介意、反對

2. call back 打電話回來

代接電話

精選例句

→ This is Dr. Smith's office.
這是史密斯辦公室。

→ I'm sorry, but he is busy with another line[1].
很抱歉,他正在忙線中。

→ Wait a moment, please. I'll get him.
請稍等,我去叫他。

→ Let me see if he is in.
我看看他在不在。

→ You can try again in a few minutes[2].
你可以過幾分鐘再打來看看。

→ Which David do you want to talk to?
你要和哪一個大衛說話?

→ Do you know his extension[3]?
你知道他的分機嗎?

→ Would you mind calling back later?
你介意稍後再打來嗎?

電話聯絡　**Phone**

精選句型

You can try again in a few minutes.

你可以過幾分鐘再打來看看。

句型

| 稍後 | in a few minutes |
| | later |

句型範例

❖ I'll finish it in a few minutes.
我幾分鐘後就會完成。

❖ She'll be here later.
她等一下就來。

Word Bank

1.be busy with another line 忙線中

2.in a few minutes 再過幾分鐘

3.extension　n. 分機

067

請對方稍候

精選例句

→ Hold on[1], please.
請稍等。

→ Just a minute, please.
請等一下。

→ Would you wait a moment, please?
能請你稍等一下嗎？

→ Could you hold the line[2], please?
能請你稍等不要掛斷電話嗎？

→ Hold the line, please.
請稍等不要掛斷電話。

→ Can you hold?
您能等嗎？

→ Let me see if he's here. Hang on[3], OK?
我看看他在不在。等一下，好嗎？

→ One moment, please. I'll see if Mr. Jones is available.
請等一下。我看看瓊斯先生有沒有空。

電話聯絡 **Phone**

精選句型

I'll see if ~

我看看~

句 型

I'll see if someone + 動詞

句型範例

❖ I'll see if he is registered.
  我看看他有沒有註冊。

❖ I'll see if he is in.
  我看看他是否在。

❖ I'll see if he is at home.
  我看看他是否在家。

Word Bank

1. hold on 等一下

2. hold the line 不要掛斷電話

3. hang on 不要掛斷電話

MP3 068

Unit 8
無法接電話

精選例句

→ Mr. Jones is on another line[1].
瓊斯先生正忙線中。

→ He is busy with another line.
他正在另一條線上（講電話）。

→ He will be back after 2 o'clock.
他會在兩點之後回來。

→ He is busy at present[2] and can't speak to you.
他現在很忙，不能跟你說話。

→ I'm sorry, but he is not at his desk[3].
很抱歉，他不在座位上。

→ I'm sorry, but he is in a meeting[4] now.
很抱歉，他現在正在開會中。

→ I'm sorry, but he just went out.
很抱歉，他剛出去。

→ I'm afraid he is not here.
他恐怕不在這裡。

電話聯絡 **Phone**

精選句型

He is busy with another line.

他正在另一條線上(講電話)。

句 型

be busy with + something

句型範例

❖ I am busy with my homework.
　我在忙功課。

❖ He is busy with love affairs.
　他在忙談戀愛。

❖ He is busy with another call.
　他在忙線中。

Word Bank

1. be on another line
　在另一線電話通話中

2. at present 目前
3. be at sb's desk 在座位上
4. meeting　n. 會議

Unit 9

轉接電話

精選例句

→ Could you put me through to Peter, please?
能幫我轉接電話給彼得嗎？

→ Would you tell her to answer[1] my call?
可以請你轉告她接我的電話嗎？

→ I'll put you through[2].
我幫你接過去。

→ I'll transfer your call[3].
我幫你轉接電話。

→ Please hold. I'll put you through.
請稍後，我幫你轉接。

→ I'll connect you.
我幫你轉接電話。

→ I'll connect you to extension 747.
我幫你轉到分機747。

→ I'll transfer your call to the marketing department.
我會幫你轉接到行銷部門。

電話聯絡 Phone

精選句型

I'll put you through.
我幫你接過去。

句型

主詞 + will + 原形動詞

句型範例

❖ I'll call you back later.
我等一下打電話給你。

❖ I'll get it.
我來接。

❖ We'll let you know.
我們會讓你知道。

Word Bank

1. answer　v. 回答電話

2. put through　轉接

3. transfer call　轉接電話

Unit 10
詢問來電者身分

精選例句

→ Who is this?
您是哪位?

→ May I ask who is calling?
請問您是哪位?

→ May I know who is calling?
請問您的大名?

→ Who is calling, please?
請問您的大名?

→ Who should I say is calling?
我要說是誰來電?

→ May I have your name, please?
請問您的大名?

→ Are you Mr. Smith?
你是史密斯先生嗎?

→ You are...?
您是…?

電話聯絡 Phone

精選句型

May I ~?

我能~?

句 型

May I + 原形動詞

句 型 範 例

✤ May I help you?
需要我協助嗎?

✤ May I have some more tea, please?
我能再多要點茶嗎?

✤ May I have you attention, please?
請各位注意一下!

✤ May I ask a question?
我能問一個問題嗎?

✤ May I make a reservation for to-morrow?
我能預約明天嗎?

✤ May I use your phone?
我能借用你的電話嗎?

Unit
11

電話約定會面

➜ Let me see my schedule[1].
我看看我的行程。

➜ When do you prefer[2]?
你想要什麼時候

➜ How about ten o'clock tomorrow?
明天十點如何？

➜ Can you come to a meeting on Friday?
你星期五能參加會議嗎？

➜ Let me check my schedule and call you back.
讓我查查我的行程再回你電話。

➜ We're planning on having it around noon[3].
我們計劃在中午舉行(會議)。

➜ If I'm not in, could you leave a message on my answering machine[4]?
如果我不在，你能留言在我的答錄機嗎？

➜ I'll tell him to be on time.
我會告訴他要準時。

電話聯絡 Phone

精選句型

How about ~?

~如何?

句型

How about + 名詞 / 動名詞

句型範例

❖ How about this Friday?
這個星期五如何?

❖ How about having dinner tonight?
今晚要不要一起吃晚餐?

Word Bank

1.schedule n. 行程

2.prefer v. 偏好

3.noon n. 中午

4.answering machine 答錄機

072

留言給對方

精選例句

→ Could I leave him a message[1]?
我能留言給他嗎？

→ Would you tell Mr. Jones David called?
能告訴瓊斯先生，大衛打過電話嗎？

→ Tell her to give me a call as soon as possible[2].
告訴她盡快回我電話。

→ Ask him to return[3] my phone.
請他回我電話。

→ This is David calling from Japan.
我是從日本打電話來的大衛。

→ Sure. My number is 8547-3663.
好的，我的號碼是 8547-3663。

→ Would you ask him to call Mark at 8547-3663?
你能請他打電話到 8547-3663 給馬克嗎？

→ Call me at 5697-1000, extension 27.
打電話到 5697-1000 分機 27 給我。

電話聯絡 **Phone**

精選句型

Tell her ~

告訴她 ~

句 型

	me	
tell +	him	+ 原形動詞
	her	名詞
	them	

句型範例

❖ Tell him to leave her alone.
告訴他離她遠一點。

❖ Tell me your thoughts.
告訴我你的想法。

Word Bank

1.leave a message　留下口信

2.as soon as possible　盡快

3.return　v. 回電

Unit 13
代為留言

➔ May I take a message[1] for him?
需要留話給他嗎？

➔ Let me take a message for you.
我幫你留個話。

➔ Yes. Go ahead, please.
可以，請說。

➔ Of course. Hold on for a second.
當然好，等一下。

➔ Let me grab[2] a pen and paper.
讓我拿個紙筆。

➔ Let me find a piece of paper to write it down[3].
讓我找張紙寫下來。

➔ Could you say that again, please?
可以請你再說一遍嗎？

➔ I'll have[4] him call you back.
我會請他回你電話。

電話聯絡 Phone

精選句型

Could you ~, please?

可以請你~嗎？

句 型

請求句型, please?

句型範例

❖ Come again, please?
　請再説一遍，好嗎？

❖ Try again, please?
　請再試一次，好嗎？

❖ Could you repeat again, please?
　能請你再説一遍，好嗎？

Word Bank

1.take a message　記口信

2.grab　v. 快取

3.write down　寫下

4.have　v. 要求

074

Unit
14

打錯電話

➤ I'm afraid you've got the wrong number.
你恐怕撥錯電話了。

➤ You must have the wrong number.
你一定是打錯號碼了。

➤ What number are you dialing[1]?
你打幾號？

➤ What number did you dial?
你打幾號？

➤ I'm calling 8647-3663.
我撥的電話是 8647-3663。

➤ Is this 8647-3663?
這是 8647-3663 嗎？

➤ There is no one here by that name.
這裡沒有這個人。

➤ There is no David here.
這裡沒有大衛這個人。

電話聯絡 Phone

精選句型

I'm sorry, but ~

很抱歉,但是~

句型

I'm sorry, but + 子句

句型範例

✤ I'm sorry, but he's in a meeting.
抱歉,但是他在會議中。

✤ I'm sorry, but he's not available.
抱歉,但是他沒有空。

✤ I am sorry but we don't have vacancy for tonight.
抱歉,但是我們今晚沒有空房。

Word Bank

1.dial　v. 撥打(電話號碼)

Unit 15

聽不清楚

精選例句

➔ I'm sorry, but I don't understand.
抱歉，我不懂。

➔ Could you repeat[1] again, please?
能請你再說一遍嗎？

➔ Pardon[2]?
你說什麼？

➔ Could you speak up[3] a little, please?
能請你說大聲一點嗎？

➔ I can't hear you very well.
我聽不清楚你說什麼。

➔ I'm afraid I can't hear you.
抱歉，我沒聽到。

➔ What did you say?
你說什麼？

➔ Could you speak slowly, please?
請說慢一點好嗎？

電話聯絡 Phone

精選句型

Pardon?
你説什麼？

句型範例

❖ I beg your pardon?
你説什麼？

❖ Come again?
你説什麼？

❖ What did you just say?
你剛剛説什麼？

Word Bank

1. repeat v. 重説

2. pardon n. 原諒（請再説一遍）

3. speak up 大聲説

電話有問題

精選例句

→ The line is very bad.
線路不太好。

→ My call did not go through[1].
我的電話並沒有撥通。

→ Could you speak louder? It's bad connection[2].
你能大聲一點嗎？線路很差。

→ I can't hear you very well.
我聽不清楚。

→ I'm afraid I can't hear you.
抱歉，我聽不見。

→ Can you hear me?
你聽得見我嗎？

→ Hello?
哈囉？（你有在聽嗎？）

→ Anybody there?
有人在聽嗎？

電話聯絡 **Phone**

精選句型

Hello?

哈囉？

句型範例

* Hello? Are you still there?
  哈囉？你還在嗎？
* Hello? Anybody home?
  哈囉？有人在嗎？
* Hello? Anyone there?
  哈囉？有人嗎？
* Hello? David? Is that you?
  哈囉？大衛？是你嗎？

Word Bank

1.go through 接通

2.connection n. 連接

Unit 17

電話無法接通

精選例句

→ Your line is always engaged[1].
你的電話一直佔線中。

→ The line is always engaged or unanswered.
電話老是佔線或是沒有人接。

→ I've tried to get through several times[2] but it's always engaged.
我試著要接通，可是一直佔線中。

→ The line was busy.
電話忙線。

→ I got the busy signals.
(對方)電話忙線。

→ He is on another line at the moment[3].
他現在正在電話中。

→ His phone is busy right now[4].
他現在正在忙線中。

電話聯絡 Phone

精選句型

I've tried to ~

我已經試著要~

句 型

have / has	+tried to + 原形動詞

句型範例

* I've tried to contact you.
  我已經試著要聯絡你。

* She has tried to escape from him.
  她已經試著要躲避他。

Word Bank

1. engaged a. （電話）佔線中

2. several times 好多次

3. at the moment 當下

4. right now 現在

Unit
18

轉告留言

精選例句

➜ I'll tell Mr. Smith that you called.
我會告訴史密斯先生你來電。

➜ I'll ask him to call you back as soon as possible.
我會請他盡快回你電話。

➜ I'll tell him as soon as he returns[1].
他回來我就會告訴他。

➜ I'll have him call you back[2].
我會請他回電給你。

➜ David called you this morning.
大衛今天早上有打電話給你。

➜ David asked you to return[3] his call.
大衛請你回他電話。

➜ David is expecting[4] your return.
大衛在等你的回電。

電話聯絡 **Phone**

精選句型

David is expecting ~
大衛在等~

句 型

| be expecting+ | something |
| | someone |

句型範例

❖ We are expecting you.
我們正在等您來。

❖ Mr. Smith is expecting you at his office.
史密斯先生在他的辦公室等你。

Word Bank

1.return   v. 回程

2.call sb. back 回某人電話

3.return   v. 回電話

4.expect   v. 預期

MP3 079

Unit 19

結束通電話

精選例句

➜ I've got to hang up[1] the phone.
我要掛電話了。

➜ I have to get going.
我要掛電話了。

➜ I'd better get off the phone[2].
我最好掛電話了。

➜ I've got to leave now.
我要走了。

➜ I'll let you go.
我要掛電話了。

➜ Thank you for calling.
謝謝你打電話來。

➜ You can call me anytime[3].
歡迎隨時打電話給我。

➜ Just give me a call when you have a chance[4].
有機會的話，打電話給我。

電話聯絡 Phone

Just give me a call.

要打電話給我。

句型範例

❖ Give me a call.
給我個電話吧！

❖ Call me.
打電話給我。

❖ Call me at the office.
打電話到我辦公室來。

❖ He phoned me the good news.
他打電話告訴我這個好消息。

Word Bank

1.hang up 掛斷電話

2.get off the phone 結束通話

3.anytime adv. 在任何時候

4.have a chance 有機會、有時間

MP3 080

有關電話的對話

精選例句

✈ I'll get it.
我來接。

✈ It's for me.
這是打給我的電話。

✈ Who called?
誰打來?

✈ Did it go through?
(電話)打通了嗎?

✈ Can you answer¹ the phone?
你能不能去接電話?

✈ Anybody answer the phone, please?
誰來接個電話吧?

✈ Can you get it, David?
大衛,你能不能去接電話?

✈ No one answered.
沒人接電話。

✈ He hung up² without saying a word.
他一句話也沒說就把電話掛了。

電話聯絡　Phone

✈ He hung up on me.
他掛我的電話。

✈ Anybody called me?
有人打電話給我嗎？

✈ I didn't get his call.
我沒有接到他的電話。

✈ Do you know his phone number?
你知道他的電話嗎？

✈ Sorry, who did you want to speak to?
抱歉，你要找誰講電話？

Word Bank

1.answer　v. 接電話

2.hang up　掛電話

Unit 21

電話常用短語

精選例句

→ Hello?
哈囉？

→ I hope I didn't disturb[1] you.
我希望我沒有打擾你。

→ I'm sorry to call you so late.
我很抱歉這麼晚打電話給你。

→ Am I calling at a bad time?
我打電話來的時間對嗎？

→ Hi, Barry. Got a minute[2] now?
嗨，貝瑞，現在有空嗎？

→ Keep going.
說吧！

→ Thank you for waiting.
謝謝你等這麼久。

→ Sorry to have kept you waiting.
抱歉讓你久等了。

→ I was just about to call you.
我剛好要打電話給您。

電話聯絡　Phone

→ Please give me his phone number.
請給我他的電話號碼。

→ Could you spell your name, please?
能請你拼一遍你的名字嗎？

→ Could you spell that, please?
能請你拼一遍嗎？

→ Does he have your number?
他知道你的號碼嗎？

→ Can you put David back on?
你能否請大衛再來聽電話呢？

→ Can you fax your enquiry to us at 8647-3663?
能請您將需求傳真到 8647-3663 給我方嗎？

Word Bank

1.disturb　v. 打擾

2.got a minute　有空閒時間

單字整理

phone call 電話

call 打電話

answer 接電話

speak 說

talk 說

dial 撥號

phone number 電話號碼

repeat 重說

hello 哈囉

speak up 大聲說

loud 大聲

hear 聽見

reach 聯絡(某人)

extension 分機

call for 來電找(某人)

put through 電話轉接

call back 回電

return 回電

return sb's call 回某人電話

busy 忙碌的

busy with another line 忙線中

電話聯絡 **Phone**

on another line 在另一線電話通話中

right now 現在

at the moment 當下

at present 目前

later 稍後

anytime 在任何時候

in a few minutes 再過幾分鐘

as soon as possible 盡快

wait 等待

wait a moment 稍候

hold on 等一下

hold the line 不要掛斷電話

hang on 不要掛斷(電話)

hang up 掛斷電話

transfer call 轉接電話

phone 電話機

answering machine 答錄機

message 留言

take a message 記口信

leave a message 留下口信

單字整理

ask 要求

inform 通知

get someone 請人來接電話

write down 寫下

go through 接通

engaged 佔線中

get off the phone 結束通話

connection 連接

line 線路

和客戶互動
Client

MP3 083

Unit
1

拜訪客戶

→ Is Mr. Smith in?
史密斯先生在嗎？

→ May I see[1] Mr. Smith?
我可以見史密斯先生嗎？

→ I'd like to see Mr. Smith.
我要見史密斯先生。

→ I'd like to meet[2] Mr. Smith.
我要見史密斯先生。

→ I'm here to see Mr. Smith.
我來這裡見史密斯先生。

→ My name is David Jones. I'm here to meet Mr. Smith.
我的名字是大衛・瓊斯。我來見史密斯先生的。

→ Mrs. Jones, can I see Mr. Smith now?
瓊斯女士，我現在能見史密斯先生嗎？

和客戶互動 **Client**

精選句型

I'm here to see ~
我來這裡見~

句 型

be here to + 原形動詞

句型範例

✤ I'm here to make it clear.
我來這裡要澄清這件事。

✤ I'm here to seek you.
我來這裡找你。

✤ I'm here to satisfy your requirements.
我來這裡滿足你的需求。

Word Bank

1.see　v. 見面

2.meet　v. 見面

MP3 084

與客戶有約

精選例句

→ I have an appointment[1] with him.
　我和他有約。

→ I have an appointment with Mr. Smith for 3 o'clock.
　我和史密斯先生三點有約。

→ It's for 2 o'clock, but I'm little early[2].
　有的，我兩點有約，但是我提早到。

→ We have a 3 o'clock appointment.
　我們約了三點鐘要見面。

→ Is Mr. Smith ready to see me?
　史密斯先生準備要見我了嗎？

→ Is Mr. Smith in his office?
　史密斯先生有在他的辦公室嗎？

→ Sorry, I'm late. Is Mr. Smith still here?
　對不起我遲到了。史密斯先生還在這裡嗎？

→ Mr. Smith invited me to meet him.
　史密斯先生邀請我來見他。

和客戶互動 **Client**

精選句型

Is he ready to ~?

他準備要~？

句型

be ready to + 原形動詞

句型範例

❖ We are ready to hold the meeting.
我們準備好要召開會議了。

❖ It's ready to launch!
準備開始了。

❖ Are you ready to beat them?
你準備好要打敗他們了嗎？

Word Bank

1.have an appointment 有約定

2.early adv. 提早

Unit 3

沒有事先預約

精選例句

→ Do you have an appointment?
您有事先約嗎？

→ No, I don't have an appointment.
沒有，我沒有事先約。

→ I don't have an appointment.
我沒有事先約。

→ May I make an appointment¹ with Mr. Smith?
能安排和史密斯先生見面嗎？

→ Would you give me an hour?
能給我一個小時的時間嗎。

→ What time is he available²?
他什麼時候有空？

→ Could you arrange a meeting with Mr. Jones for me?
能請你幫我安排和瓊斯先生的會面嗎？

和客戶互動 **Client**

精選句型

Would you give me an hour?

能給我一個小時的時間嗎？

句型

give + | me
him/her
them/us
you | + 名詞

句型範例

❖ Just give me a chance.
只要給我一個機會。

❖ Why don't you give him a job?
你為什麼不給他一個工作？

Word Bank

1. make an appointment 安排會面

2. available a. 有空的

086

說明來訪目的

精選例句

→ Why do you wish to see him?
您為什麼要見他？

→ It's about a new contract[1].
是有關新合約的事。

→ He invited me to this meeting.
他邀請我參加這場會議。

→ We are supposed to[2] meet at five.
我們原本預計五點見面的。

→ I was wondering[3] if he is interested in[4] our products.
我是在想他是否對我們的商品有興趣？

→ Can you tell him I'm here to discuss[5] sales promotions?
你能告訴他我是來這裡討論行銷計畫嗎？

→ We are here to attend the meeting.
我們來這裡參加會議。

和客戶互動 Client

精選句型

Why do you wish to see him?

您為什麼要見他？

句型

wish + 名詞受詞 + 形容詞 to 動詞

to 動詞

句型範例

* I wish everything ready.
  我希望一切準備妥當。
* What do you wish me to do?
  你想要我做什麼？

Word Bank

1. contract　n. 合約
2. be supposed to　原訂要
3. wondering　a. 疑惑的
4. be interested in...　對⋯有興趣
5. discuss　v. 討論

087

精選例句

➥ May I have your name, please?
請問您的大名？

➥ I'm Betty Jones.
我是貝蒂・瓊斯。

➥ Hi, I'm David Jones from Taiwan.
嗨，我是來自台灣的大衛・瓊斯。

➥ I came from London.
我來自倫敦。

➥ David White of BCQ Company.
(我是) BCQ 的大衛・懷特。

➥ David Jones. I called on[1] Mr. Lee yesterday.
我是大衛・瓊斯。昨天我拜訪過李先生。

➥ I'm Betty, and this is my co-worker[2] David.
我是貝蒂這位是我同事大衛。

和客戶互動 **Client**

精選句型

This is my co-worker David.

這位是我的同事大衛。

句型

This is + 身分 + 人名

句型範例

* This is my roommate Joan.
  這位是我的室友瓊安。

* This is her boss Mr. Jones.
  這位是她的老闆瓊斯先生。

* This is David's sister Mary.
  這位是大衛的姊姊瑪莉。

Word Bank

1.call on 拜訪

2.co-worker n. 同事

問候客戶

→ Hello, David, how are you?
哈囉，大衛，你好嗎？

→ It's nice to meet you, Mr. Jones.
瓊斯先生，很高興與你見面。

→ How is your business[1]?
生意好嗎？

→ How have you been?
近來好嗎？

→ How were your weeks?
這幾個星期過得如何？

→ How is your family?
你的家人好嗎？

→ Please say hello to Jane for me.
幫我向珍問候。

→ What are you working on[2]?
你在忙些什麼？

和客戶互動 **Client**

精選句型

How is your business?

生意好嗎？

句 型

How + be 動詞 + | 人名 |
| 身份 |
| 事件 |
| 過程 |

句型範例

❖ How is John?
約翰好嗎？

❖ How was your flight?
您一路上順利吧？

Word Bank

1.business n. 生意

2.work on 致力於

Unit
7

客套用語

精選例句

→ Thank you for inviting[1] me.
感謝你的邀請。

→ Thank you for your time.
感謝您的撥冗。

→ You look busy.
你看起來好像很忙！

→ It's been a long time.
好久不見。

→ I'm happy to meet you.
很高興見到你。

→ I'm glad to see you again.
很高興再次見到你。

→ It's nice meeting you, too.
我也很高興認識你。

→ It's my honor[2] to see you.
能見到你是我的榮幸。

和客戶互動 Client

精選句型

You look busy.
你看起來好像很忙！

句型

You look + 形容詞

句型範例

* You look pale.
你看起來好像很蒼白。

* You look terrible.
你看起來好像很糟糕。

* You look great.
你看起來很好。

Word Bank

1.inviting n. 邀請

2.honor n. 榮幸

MP3 090

Unit
8

洽談公事

精選例句

→ I need to talk with you about our plans.
我需要和您談談我們的計畫。

→ How would you like to solve this problem[1]?
您要如何解決這個問題？

→ I think we will take the responsibility[2].
我覺得我們會負責。

→ We hope you will consider[3] it.
我們希望你能考慮它。

→ It's a great offer[4], isn't it?
這是一個很好的提案，不是嗎？

→ Do you mind if we make suggestions[5]?
您介意我們提建議嗎？

→ We need to talk about the details[6].
我們需要討論有關細節的事。

→ We are offering a special plan.
我們提供一份促銷的提議。

和客戶互動 Client

精選句型

It's a great offer, isn't it?

這是一個很好的提案,不是嗎?

句型

be 動詞 ~, | isn't it?
| right?

※ be 動詞所引導的肯定句

句型範例

❧ It's great, isn't it?
這很好,不是嗎?

❧ She is smart, right?
她很聰明,對吧?

Word Bank

1.solve this problem 解決這個問題
2.responsibility n. 責任
3.consider v. 考慮
4.offer v. 提議
5.suggestion n. 建議
6.detail n. 細節

確認身分

→ Excuse me, are you Mr. Smith?
抱歉，請問你是史密斯先生嗎？

→ Are you Mr. Smith?
您是史密斯先生嗎？

→ Mr. Smith?
史密斯先生？

→ May I have your name, please?
請問您的大名？

→ Are you Mr. Smith of BCM?
您是 BCM 公司的史密斯先生嗎？

→ Mr. Smith? Here[1]!
史密斯先生？在這裡！

→ I'm David Jones of CNS Company.
我是 CNS 公司的大衛・瓊斯。

→ How do you do? I'm David Jones.
你好嗎？我是大衛・瓊斯。

和客戶互動 Client

精選句型

Mr. Smith? Here!

史密斯先生？在這裡！

句型範例

❖ David? I am here!
大衛？我在這裡！

❖ David? Over here!
大衛？在這裡！

❖ It's ten o'clock and here is the news.
現在十點鐘，新聞開始了。

Word Bank

1.here adv. 在這裡

MP3 092

Unit 10

招待客戶

精選例句

→ Just a minute, please.
請等一下。

→ Sit down please, Mr. Smith.
請坐,史密斯先生。

→ Would you like a cup of tea?
您要喝杯茶嗎?

→ Can I get you some coffee?
你要喝咖啡嗎?

→ Can I get you something to drink?
您要喝點什麼嗎?

→ Would you give me your business card[1]?
能給我一張名片嗎?

→ Make yourself comfortable[2].
不要拘束!

和客戶互動 **Client**

【精選句型】

Make yourself comfortable.

不要拘束！

句 型

make someone + | 形容詞
| 冠詞 + 身分名詞

句型範例

✤ Make yourself happy.
讓自己快樂！

✤ Make yourself a millionaire.
讓自己成為百萬富翁。

2 0 5

Word Bank

1.business card 名片

2.make yourself comfortable 不要拘束

引導訪客方位

➤ Please come on in.
請進!

➤ Just follow[1] me, please.
請跟我來。

➤ This way, please.
請走這裡。

➤ His office is just through those doors.
他的辦公室穿過那些門就到了。

➤ Please take the elevator[2] on your left to the seventh floor.
請搭您左手邊的電梯到七樓。

➤ This is our conference room.
這是我們的會議室。

➤ That is our Vice President's office.
那是我們副總裁的辦公室。

和客戶互動 Client

精選句型

Please take the elevator on your left.

請搭您左手邊的電梯。

❖ take medicine/temperature

吃藥/量體溫

❖ take pictures

拍照

❖ take a train/bus/taxi

搭火車/公車/計程車

❖ take a walk/bath

散步/洗澡

Word Bank

1. follow v. 跟隨

2. elevator n. 電梯

MP3 094

Unit 12

主管的現況

精選例句

✈ Mr. Jones is expecting[1] you.
瓊斯先生正在等您來。

✈ Mr. Jones can see you now.
瓊斯先生現在可以見您。

✈ Mr. Jones is in conference.
瓊斯先生正在開會。

✈ He is in the middle of something[2].
他正在忙。

✈ He can't see you now.
他現在無法見您。

✈ I'm sorry, but he is not in now.
抱歉，但是他現在不在。

✈ He will be here very soon.
他很快就會來了。

✈ He will see you in a minute[3].
他馬上就會來見你。

和客戶互動 Client

精選句型

He will see you in a minute.

他馬上就會來見你。

句 型

馬上	in a minute right away soon very soon

句型範例

❖ I'll get started right away.
  我馬上開始。

❖ He will be back very soon.
  他很快就會回來。

Word Bank

1.expect v. 期待

2.in the middle of something 忙碌中

3.in a minute 馬上

傳達轉告來訪

精選例句

→ Let me call Mr. Jones to come over[1].
我去叫瓊斯先生過來。

→ I'll call Mr. Jones's office.
我會打電話到瓊斯先生的辦公室。

→ I'll tell Mr. Jones you are here.
我會告訴瓊斯先生您來了！

→ Let me see if Mr. Jones is available[2].
我看看瓊斯先生有沒有空。

→ Please wait a moment. I'll inform Mr. Jones that you're here.
請等一下，我來通知瓊斯先生你的來訪。

→ Mr. Smith, Mr. White is expecting[3] you.
史密斯先生，懷特先生正在等您來！

→ I'll inform[4] Mr. Jones right now.
我現在馬上通知瓊斯先生。

和客戶互動 **Client**

(精選句型)

Mr. Jones is available.
瓊斯先生有空。

句型

someone / something	+ be 動詞 + available

句型範例

❖ I'm not sure if he is available.
我不確定他是否有空。

❖ Let me see if he is available.
我看看他是否有空。

❖ Is there any rooms available?
有沒有任何空房間?

Word Bank

1. come over 過來

2. available a. 有空閒的

3. expect v. 期待

4. inform v. 通知

096

歡迎/問候

精選例句

➔ Welcome, Mr. Taylor.
泰勒先生，歡迎你！

➔ On behalf of[1] our company, I'd like to welcome[2] all of our visitors[3].
我代表本公司歡迎各位來訪。

➔ Good morning/afternoon/evening.
早安/午安/晚安。

➔ How are you?
你好嗎？

➔ Hi, John, what have you been doing?
嗨，約翰，最近都在忙些什麼？

➔ How do you do?
你好嗎？

➔ How's everything going?
一切都好嗎？

➔ How have you been?
近來好嗎？

和客戶互動 Client

精選句型

Welcome, Mr. Taylor.
泰勒先生，歡迎你！

句型範例

✤ Welcome!
歡迎！

✤ Welcome to Taiwan.
歡迎到台灣！

✤ Welcome back to Taiwan.
歡迎回到台灣！

✤ Welcome your comments.
歡迎你的評論！

Word Bank

1. on behalf of 代表

2. welcome v. 歡迎

3. visitor n. 訪客

MP3 097

Unit 15

和訪客寒暄

精選例句

→ How was your flight?
您一路上順利吧？

→ Have you recovered[1] from the journey[2]?
是否已從旅途的疲勞中回復過來？

→ How long do you intend to stay in the USA?
您打算在美國停留多久？

→ What's the main purpose of your visit?
您來訪的主要目的是什麼？

→ What do you think of Taiwan?
您對台灣的印象如何？

→ I hope you had a good sleep last night.
希望你昨晚睡得好。

→ I have longed to meet you.
久仰大名。

→ You haven't changed at all.
你一點都沒變。

和客戶互動 Client

精選句型

What do you think of~?

您對~的印象如何?

句型

think of + | someone
| something

句型範例

❖ What do you think of Joyce?
你覺得喬伊斯如何?

❖ What do you think?
你認為呢?

❖ What do you think, my friend?
我的朋友,你覺得如何?

Word Bank

1.recover v. 復原

2.journey n. 旅行

結束招待

→ Thank you for coming.
感謝來訪。

→ Have a nice day.
祝你有美好的一天。

→ Have a good night.
祝你晚上愉快。

→ Thank you for everything.
感謝您所做的一切。

→ How nice to see you again.
很高興再次見到你。

→ Let's get together[1] again sometime[2].
有空再找個時間聚一聚。

→ Good night.
晚安！（道別用語）

和客戶互動 Client

精選句型

How nice to see you again.

很高興再次見到你。

句型

How + 形容詞 +
| to + 原形動詞 |
| 主詞 + 一般動詞 |

句型範例

❖ How great to find so many students.
能找到這麼多學生真好！

❖ How smart you are.
你真聰明！

❖ How chilly it is.
真冷！

Word Bank

1. get together 聚會

2. sometime 日後、改天

MP3 099

Unit
17

行程安排

✈ Where do you want to visit[1] tomorrow morning?
明天上午你想要去哪裡參訪？

✈ What is your opinion[2] about the schedule of the next six days?
接下來的六天行程您有何意見？

✈ What do you think of this arrangement[3]?
這樣的安排您覺得如何？

✈ How about the following[4] Friday?
接下來的週五如何？

✈ Is there anything else you'd like to achieve[5] on this visit?
這次來訪你們還有其他事要處理嗎？

✈ Can we make it on Friday next week?
我們可以安排在下週五嗎？

和客戶互動 **Client**

精選句型

How about ~?

~你覺得如何？

句 型

| 助動詞 + 主詞 + 動詞 |

How + about + 名詞 / 動詞 ing

句型範例

❖ How do you like it?
   你喜歡嗎？

❖ How about going out for a drink?
   要不要去喝一杯？

❖ How about it?
   這個如何？

Word Bank

1. visit   v. 拜見、參觀
2. opinion   n. 意見
3. arrangement   n. 安排
4. following   a. 接下來的
5. achieve   v. 完成

100

精選例句

→ I'm not certain[1] if I'll be free on that day.
我還不確定那一天是否有空。

→ I'd love to meet you for lunch.
我很樂意與你共進午餐。

→ Thank you for taking all the trouble to arrange the schedule for my visit.
感謝您費心安排我的來訪行程。

→ I'll be very happy to join you.
我很樂意參加。

→ We will be most delighted[2] to meet him.
我們非常高興去拜見他。

→ I'll come for you at 2:00 this afternoon.
我會在下午兩點去接你。

→ We'll be waiting for you in the lobby[3] downstairs[4].
我們會在樓下的大廳等你。

和客戶互動 Client

精選句型

I'd love to meet you for lunch.

我很樂意與你共進午餐。

句型

主詞 + would love to + 原形動詞

句型範例

♣ I'd love to go with you.
我很樂意和你去。

♣ I'd love to visit Mr. Jones.
我願意去拜訪瓊斯先生。

Word Bank

1. certain   a. 確定的

2. delighted   a. 高興的

3. lobby   n. 大廳

4. downstairs   adv. 在樓下

Unit 19
安排會議

精選例句

→ Let's kick off[1] the meeting at 10 o'clock.
我們十點鐘召開會議。

→ I'll arrange a staff[2] meeting.
我會安排一場員工會議。

→ Can we set[3] the date for the next meeting?
我們可以安排下一次會議的日期嗎？

→ The next meeting will be on next Friday.
下一次的會議會在下星期五。

→ We'll hold the meeting[4] in Room 301.
我們會在301會議室召開會議。

→ We will fix a meeting[5] next week to discuss the budget.
我們會在下週安排討論預算的會議。

→ When will you be available?
你什麼時候有空？

和客戶互動 Client

精選句型

We'll fix a meeting.

我們會安排會議。

句型

| fix
call
arrange | + a meeting |

句型範例

❖ We'll fix a meeting tomorrow.
我們明天會安排一場會議。

❖ I should call a meeting.
我應該召開一場會議。

❖ I arranged a meeting yesterday.
我昨天安排一場會議。

Word Bank

1.kick off 開始
2.staff n. 員工
3.set v. 安排
4.hold the meeting 舉行會議
5.fix a meeting 舉行會議

MP3 102

邀請客戶

精選例句

→ Will you come along¹ with me?
你願意和我一起來嗎？

→ Would you like to join² us?
你要加入我們嗎？

→ Do you have any plans on Sunday?
您週日有任何計畫嗎？

→ Will you be free on this Friday?
您本週五是否有空？

→ Mr. Jones invites you to attend³ our annual⁴ party.
瓊斯先生邀請您出席我們的年度宴會。

→ Why don't you join us?
何不加入我們？

→ Would you like to have dinner with us?
要不要和我們一起吃晚餐？

→ I really want you to come over.
我真心希望您能過來。

和客戶互動 **Client**

精選句型

Why don't you ~?

何不~?

句型

Why + | don't you/we/they ~
| doesn't he/she ~

句型範例

❖ Why don't you come over here?
你怎麼不來?

❖ Why doesn't he call for help?
他為什麼不要求幫忙?

Word Bank

1.come along 一起來

2.join v. 加入

3.attend v. 參加

4.annual a. 年度的

103

Unit
21
參觀公司

精選例句

→ Let me show[1] you our office.
我來帶你們參觀我們的辦公室。

→ Would you be interested in[2] visiting BCQ Company?
您是否有興趣參觀 BCQ 公司？

→ This is our sales marketing department[3].
這是我們的市場行銷部門。

→ That is Mr. White's office.
那是懷特先生的辦公室。

→ Down there is our conference room[4].
盡頭那是我們的會議室。

→ Our staff is working all around here.
我們的人員都在這裡工作。

→ Is it possible for you to visit our factories?
你們要不要參觀我們工廠？

和客戶互動 Client

精選句型

Let me show you ~
我來帶你們參觀~

句型

Let + 受詞 + 原形動詞

句型範例

✤ Let me be your friend.
讓我當你的朋友。

✤ Let him make comments.
讓他發表言論。

✤ Let us pray for her.
讓我們為她禱告！

Word Bank

1.show v. 展示

2.be interested in 對~有興趣

3.sales marketing department 行銷部

4.conference room 會議室

單字整理

🎵 104

see 見面
meet 見面
have an appointment 有約定
appointment 約定
early 提早
late 遲到
make an appointment 安排會面
available 有空的
discuss 討論
meeting 會面
call on 拜訪
visitor 訪客
visit 拜見、參觀
arrange 安排
invite 邀請
consider 考慮
offer 提議
suggest 建議
join 加入
attend 參加
expect 期待

和客戶互動 Client

inform 通知

staff 員工

co-worker 同事

boss 老闆

manager 經理

in person 本人親自

business 生意

solve 解決

problem 問題

responsibility 責任

detail 細節

welcome 歡迎

receive 接待

opinion 意見

idea 點子

thought 想法

arrangement 安排

drop by 順便拜訪

come over 過來

client 顧客

單字整理

customer 顧客

parent company 母公司

subsidiary 子公司

company 公司

office 辦公室

factory 工廠

overseas 海外

domestic 國內

department 部門

Chapter

6

會議

Conference

開場白

精選例句

→ Good morning/afternoon, everyone.
大家早安/午安！

→ Welcome, everyone.
歡迎各位！

→ I'm so glad to see you here on time.
很高興看見你們準時出席。

→ I'd like to thank David for coming over from Taiwan.
感謝大衛遠從台灣而來。

→ Thank you all for attending.
謝謝你們參加（會議）。

→ Unfortunately[1], Mr. Baker will not be with us today.
很遺憾貝克先生無法參加今天的會議。

→ This is my first time to attend this conference.
這是我第一次參加這個會議。

→ Thank you for inviting us.
謝謝你們邀請我們。

會議 Conference

精選句型

This is my first time to ~
這是我第一次~

句 型

序數 + time + to + 原形動詞

※序數

frist	第一的	fourth	第四的
second	第二的	fifth	第五的
third	第三的	sixth	第六的

句型範例

❖ This is my first time to attend it.
這是我第一次參加。

Word Bank

1.unfortunately　adv. 不幸地

MP3 106

歡迎參加

精選例句

→ Thank you for your attending.
感謝各位參加。

→ Good to see you again.
很高興再見到各位。

→ Welcome to this conference.
歡迎參加這場會議。

→ I'd like to welcome you all to our meeting.
歡迎各位參加這場會議。

→ I'm happy to see you here.
很高興在這裡看到各位。

→ It's a great pleasure to welcome you to this meeting.
很高興能在這場會議中歡迎各位。

→ It's a pleasure to have this opportunity[1] to discuss[2] it.
很高興有此機會討論。

會議 Conference

精選句型

It's a great pleasure ~

很高興~

句型

It's a pleasure +
| to + 原形動詞 |
| 動詞 ing |

句型範例

❖ It's a pleasure to work with you.
很高興和你一起共事。

❖ It's a pleasure talking with you.
很高興和你說話。

Word Bank

1.opportunity   n. 機會

2.discuss   v. 討論

宣佈會議開始

✈ Shall we begin[1]?
開始好嗎？

✈ Let's begin, shall we?
會議開始，好嗎？

✈ We'd better start[2].
我們最好開始(開會議)。

✈ OK, let's get started.
好了，我們開始吧！

✈ It's time to begin.
應該開始(討論)了。

✈ It's about time to begin.
時間到了，我們應該開始了。

✈ Let's get down to[3] business.
開始討論正事了。

✈ If we are all here, let's get started.
如果全都到齊，(會議)就開始。

精選句型

It's time to begin.

應該開始了。

句型

It's time to + 原形動詞

句型範例

* It's time to go home.
  回家的時間到了。

* It's time to learn English.
  學英語的時間到了。

* It's time to have fun.
  好好享樂的時間到了。

Word Bank

1. begin v. 開始

2. start v. 開始

3. get down to 開始認真對待

108

責任分配

精選例句

→ Who will keep the minutes?
誰要做會議記錄？

→ Susan has agreed to take the minutes[1].
蘇姍答應要做會議紀錄。

→ Debby, would you mind taking the minutes for the meeting?
黛比，妳介意做會議記錄嗎？

→ Maria, would you mind taking notes[2] today?
瑪麗亞，妳介意記錄今天的備忘錄嗎？

→ Are all the audio-visual aids[3] ready?
所有視聽設備都準備好了嗎？

→ David will lead point 1, Joy point 2, and Mr. White point 3.
大衛要主持第一點，喬伊第二點，懷特先生第三點。

會議 **Conference**

精選句型

Who will ~?

誰要~?

句 型

Who will + 原形動詞

※未來式句型

句型範例

* Who will tell him the truth?
  誰要告訴他實話?

* Who will be there on time?
  誰會準時到那裡?

Word Bank

1.take the minutes 擔任會議記錄

2.take notes 紀錄

3.audio-visual aid 視聽設備

Unit 5

議程安排

精選例句

→ On the agenda[1], you'll see there are four items[2].
在議程上，你會看見有四個議題。

→ First~, second~, finally~.
第一個是~，第二個是~，最後一個是~

→ Do you all have a copy of[3] the agenda?
你們都有一份今天的議程嗎？

→ Has everyone received[4] a copy of the annual project?
每個人都有收到一份年度計畫嗎？

→ Let's preview[5] the agenda.
我們先看一下議程。

→ If you don't mind, I'd like to go in order[6] today.
如果各位不建議，今天就照順序討論。

→ Let's skip item 1 and move on to item 2.
我們跳過議程一，直接進行議程二。

會 議 Conference

精選句型

I'd like to go in order.

就照順序討論。

句 型

- in order 按順序
- in order to 為了

句型範例

❖ Does it works in order?
有按照順序運轉嗎？

❖ In order to get the job, I'll do my best.
為了得到那份工作，我會盡力。

Word Bank

1.agenda　n. 議程
2.item　n. 項目
3.a copy of 一份~
4.receive　v. 收到
5.preview　v. 預覽
6.in order 按順序

110

Unit
6
會議時間

精選例句

→ There will be five minutes for each [1] item.
每一個議題有五分鐘（時間）。

→ Everybody has five minutes for each idea.
每一個人有五分鐘的時間説明每個點子。

→ David will open with five-minute introduction [2].
大衛會先做五分鐘的介紹。

→ The meeting will last [3] one hour.
會議將進行一個小時。

→ The meeting will finish [4] at three o'clock.
會議將進行到三點。

→ I hope the meeting can be finished by 4 o'clock.
我希望會議可以在四點結束。

→ Let's aim [5] for a 3:00 finish.
讓我們預計在三點結束。

會議 Conference

Let's aim for a 3:00 finish.

讓我們預計在三點結束。

句 型

Let us + 原形動詞

※ Let us=Let's

句型範例

- ✤ Let's go.
  我們走!
- ✤ Let's be friends.
  讓我們當朋友吧!

Word Bank

1. each   a. 每一個
2. introduction   n. 介紹
3. last   v. 持續
4. finish   v. 結束
5. aim   v. 致力~

111

Unit 7
會議主題

精選例句

→ Now we come to the question of the pricing policy.
現在我們進行有關價格策略的問題。

→ I'd suggest we start with the advertisement[1].
我建議從廣告開始。

→ We are here to discuss how we can improve[2] the program.
我們在這裡是要討論如何更新程式。

→ We have to come to an agreement[3] about the annual plan.
我們必須要針對年度計畫達成共識。

→ Our main aim today is to talk about the design[4] of summer catalogue.
我們今天的主要目的是討論夏季型錄的設計。

→ The reason why we are here is to discuss the sales plans.
我們在這裡的原因,是為了討論促銷計畫。

會議 Conference

The reason why we are here is ~

我們在這裡的原因是~

句 型

The reason (why) ~ + 子句 + be 動詞

※ why 可以省略不用

句型範例

* The reason we are here is to discus it.
  我們在這的原因是要討論它。

* The reason you called me is because of love.
  你是因為愛才打電話給我的。

Word Bank

1. advertisement n. 廣告

2. improve v. 改進

3. agreement n. 同意

4. design n. 設計

112

Unit 8

議題討論

精選例句

→ Shall we get down to business?
要不要就主題來討論？

→ Can you tell us how the sales project is progressing[1]?
你可以告訴我們銷售計畫的進度如何嗎？

→ How is the CSR project coming along?
客戶服務計畫進行得如何？

→ First, let's go over[2] the report.
首先，我們先瀏覽一遍報告。

→ Here are the minutes from our last[3] meeting.
這裡有一份我們上次的會議記錄。

→ First of all, we have to discuss[4] the pricing policy[5].
首先，我們必須討論價格策略。

→ If there is nothing else we need to discuss, let's move on to today's agenda.
如果沒有其他需要討論的，就繼續今天的議程。

會議 Conference

精選句型

get down to ~

就~來討論

句 型

get down to + | someone / something

句型範例

❖ Let's get down to the heart of the matter.

讓我們討論重點吧！

❖ He got down to his work after the holidays.

度假之後他開始專心工作。

Word Bank

1. progress v. 進行

2. go over 重溫

3. last a. 上一次的

4. discuss v. 討論

5. policy n. 策略

113

討論新議題

→ The next item is ~
下一個議題是~

→ The final[1] item is ~
最後一個議題是~

→ Let's begin with the first item.
先從第一個議題開始討論。

→ Let's begin with the design.
我們先從設計開始討論。

→ Are there any discussions[2] on this?
這個還有要討論的嗎？

→ Let's move on to the next item.
我們進行下一個議題。

→ What's next?
下一個(要討論)是什麼？

→ The next item on today's agenda is our services[3].
今天議程的下一個議題是有關我們的服務。

會議 Conference

精選句型

Are there any discussions?

還有要討論的嗎?

句 型

Be 動詞 + there any +

| 複數可數名詞 |
| 不可數名詞 |

※ be 動詞 are 接複數可數名詞,is 接單
數不可數名詞

句型範例

❧ Are there any English words?
還有任何英文單字嗎?

❧ Is there any sugar in the bottle?
罐子裡還有糖嗎?

Word Bank

1.final a. 最後的

2.discussion n. 討論

3.service n. 服務

腦力激盪

精選例句

➔ Don't hold back.
儘管說出來不要保留。

➔ I have got an idea.
我有一個主意。

➔ I have a few ideas I'd like to share with you.
我有一些點子,希望和各位分享。

➔ I've called this meeting to make ideas for effective promotion.
我召開這次會議,是希望為我們的促銷想一些點子。

➔ All right, we have a lot of good ideas.
好了,我們有很多很好的主意。

➔ We need some creative[1] ideas.
我們需要一些有創意的點子。

➔ Here are my suggestions.
以下是我的建議。

➔ Come on, guys, use your head[2].
拜託,各位,動動你們的腦袋。

會議 Conference

精選句型

I have a few ideas.

我有一些點子。

句 型

a few + 複數名詞

句型範例

❖ I have a few questions.
我有一些問題。

❖ I have a few favorite artists.
我有一些喜愛的藝術家。

❖ Let me make a few comments.
讓我來發表一些言論。

Word Bank

1.creative   a. 創造性的

2.use your head 動動腦

115

Unit 11

鼓勵發言

➔ Please go on.
請繼續(説下去)。

➔ Shall we start with Mr. Jones?
我們先從瓊斯先生開始好嗎？

➔ Would you like to introduce[1] this item?
你要介紹這個議題嗎？

➔ David, would you like to kick off?
大衛，可以從你開始嗎？

➔ We can't all speak at once. One at a time.
我們無法人人都同時發言。一個一個來。

➔ Would you like to open the discussion[2]?
你要先開始討論嗎？

➔ What's on your mind[3]?
你的想法呢？

➔ David, you have to speak out.
大衛，你要説出實在的話啊！

會議 Conference

精選句型

Please go on.

請繼續。

句型

go on + 介系詞~
動詞 ing

句型範例

❖ If he goes on like this he'll lose his job.
如果他繼續這樣下去,他會丟掉他的工作的。

❖ Why do you go on talking?
你為什麼一直說話?

Word Bank

1.introduce　v. 介紹

2.discussion　n. 討論

3.on your mind　想法

116

提醒注意

✈ Attention[1], please.
請注意!

✈ May I have you attention, please?
請各位注意一下!

✈ Listen to me now.
現在聽我説。

✈ Be quiet[2].
安靜。

✈ Ladies and gentlemen!
各位先生、女士!

✈ Excuse me!
抱歉!(聽我説!)

✈ Everybody, listen.
各位,聽著!

會議 Conference

精選句型

Be quiet.

安靜。

句 型

Be + 形容詞

※此為祈使句型

句型範例

✤ Be smart.

放聰明點！

✤ Be yourself.

當你自己！

Word Bank

1.attention　n. 注意力

2.quiet　a. 安靜的

117

詢問意見

精選例句

➤ What do you suggest, David?
大衛，你的建議呢？

➤ We need to go into this in more detail.
我們需要再仔細討論。

➤ Could you elaborate[1] on your point?
你可以解釋一下你的重點嗎？

➤ Any comments[2]?
有任何意見嗎？

➤ I appreciate[3] your advice.
我很想聽聽您的意見。

➤ It sounds good to me. What do you two
think of it?
聽起來很不錯，你們兩位覺得怎樣？

➤ Say something, gentlemen.
各位，說說話呀！

➤ Good question.
好問題。

會議 Conference

精選句型

I appreciate your advice.

我很想聽聽您的意見。

句型

appreciate + 善意的事件
善意的人

句型範例

❖ I appreciate your kindness.
感謝你的善意。

❖ I appreciate you, and what you have done.
感謝你和你所做的事。

Word Bank

1. elaborate v. 詳盡闡述

2. comment n. 建議

3. appreciate v. 感激

Unit 14

發表個人言論

精選例句

→ In my opinion, ~
依我的觀念，~

→ Personally, I think ~
依個人的觀念，我認為，~

→ I have a point to add[1].
我有一個重點要補充。

→ Could I comment[2] on that?
我能就這點發表言論嗎？

→ I'd like to show you my point.
我要說明一下我的論點。

→ But I have to explain[3].
但是我一定要解釋一下。

→ According to[4] our new research, ~
根據我們的最新研究，~

→ Actually, I have no idea about it.
其實，我對這件事一點也不知道。

會議 Conference

精選句型

According to ~,

根據~,

句型

according to + 名詞

句型範例

❖ According to her, Tom called at noon.
據她說,湯姆在中午有打電話來。

❖ I divided them into three groups according to age.
我按他們的年齡分成三組。

Word Bank

1.add   v. 補充

2.comment   v. 發表意見

3.explain   v. 解釋

4.according to 根據

Unit
15

會議上插話

精選例句

→ May I have a word?
我能説話嗎？

→ May I ask a question?
我能問一個問題嗎？

→ Excuse me for interrupting[1].
抱歉，我要插話。

→ Excuse me, may I ask for clarification[2] on this?
抱歉，我能在這一點上做個説明嗎？

→ Just a moment. Can we come back to you later?
請稍等。我們能夠等一下再輪到你嗎？

→ Sorry to interrupt, can we let Mark finish?
抱歉插話一下，我們可以讓馬克先説完嗎？

→ I have a question.
我有一個問題。

會議 Conference

精選句型

Excuse me for interrupting.

抱歉,我要插話。

句型

Excuse me for + 名詞 / 動詞 ing / 動詞 ing + something

句型範例

❖ Excuse me for my helpless.
原諒我幫不上忙。

❖ Excuse me for not being there.
抱歉我不在那裡。

❖ Excuse me for doing this to you.
抱歉對你做這件事。

Word Bank

1.interrupt v. 打斷(講話或講話人)

2.clarification n. 澄清

Unit
16

休息時間

精選例句

→ We are going to take a ten-minute break[1].
我們將要休息十分鐘。

→ Let's take a five-minute break.
讓我們休息五分鐘。

→ We should break[2] for coffee now.
我們現在應該休息一下。

→ I think it's time to take a break.
我想，該是休息一下了。

→ We have an intermission[3] until 4 pm.
我們暫停到下午四點。

→ It's time for a cup of coffee.
該是休息的時間了。

→ We won't have any intermission.
我們不會暫停（休息）。

→ We'll resume[4] our meeting at 4 pm.
我們下午四點鐘會重新開始我們的會議。

會議 Conference

精選句型

It's time for a cup of coffee.

該是休息的時間了。

句 型

It's time for +

名詞
someone + to + 原型動詞

句型範例

* ❖ It's time for breakfast.
  該吃早餐了。

* ❖ It's time for school.
  該上學了。

* ❖ It's time for you to grow up.
  你該長大了。

Word Bank

1.break　n. 休息

2.break　v. 休息

3.intermission　n. 中斷、暫停

4.resume　v. 繼續

Unit
17

繼續會議

精選例句

→ Shall we continue?
繼續（進行討論）好嗎？

→ Let's come back to this issue[1].
我們再回到這個議題上。

→ I think we've covered everything.
我認為我們已經涵蓋到每一件事了。

→ It looks as we've covered the main items.
看來我們已經都討論過主要議題了。

→ Shall we leave that item?
這個議題要不要就到此結束？

→ Why don't we move on to the third item instead[2]?
我們為什麼不先改為進行第三個議題？

→ Is there any other business?
還有其他事嗎？

→ Is there anything else to discuss?
還有沒有任何要討論的？

會議 Conference

精選句型

I think ~

我認為~

句　型

I think + 子句

句型範例

✤ I think we should go.
我覺得我們應該去。

✤ I think you are right.
我覺得你是對的。

Word Bank

1. issue　n. 議題

2. instead　adv. 作為替代

Unit 18

結束議題

精選例句

→ That's everything on the agenda.
這就是議程上所有的事了。

→ That's enough[1] for this item now.
這個議題討論到現在也夠了。

→ That's all for the summer promotion.
有關夏季促銷就這些囉！

→ I'll have to bring this point to a close.
這個議題就先結束囉！

→ I guess[2] nobody has anything else to say.
我猜沒有人有其他事要說吧！

→ We'll leave this point now and move on to the next item.
現在這一點就先這樣,先進行下一個議題。

→ That's enough for this item.
這個議題討論到此就夠了。

會議 Conference

精選句型

That's enough for this item.

這個議題到此就夠了。

句型

be 動詞 + enough + | for + 名詞
| to + 原形動詞

句型範例

❖ It's enough for anybody.
對任何人來說都夠了。

❖ It's enough to support you.
支持你已經夠了。

Word Bank

1. enough a. 足夠的

2. guess v. 猜測

Unit
19

總結

精選例句

→ Let me just summarize[1] my ideas.
讓我總結我的點子。

→ Let me quickly summarize what we've done today.
讓我快速總結一下今天討論的！

→ Let me go over today's main points.
讓我很快地再確認今天的重點。

→ To sum up[2], send our clients the latest catalogue.
總而言之，要寄給我們的客戶最新的型錄。

→ In brief[3], we have to cut costs[4] by one third.
總而言之，我們必須要將成本削減三分之一。

→ We have made good progress[5] today.
我們今天很有進展。

→ We'll carry on[6] our discussion tomorrow.
我們明天將繼續討論。

會議 Conference

精選句型

In brief, ~

總而言之，~

句型

總而言之，~
In short, ~
In brief, ~
In conclusion, ~

句型範例

* In short, you have never done it right.
  總而言之，你沒把事情做好。

* In brief, I would like to learn more about it.
  總而言之，我想要多學一點。

Word Bank

1. summarize v. 總結
2. sum up 總而言之
3. in brief 總而言之
4. cut cost 縮減成本
5. progress n. 進步
6. carry on 繼續

MP3 124

Unit
20

詢問對會議的瞭解

精選例句

→ Do you understand everything?
你們都明白嗎？

→ Is everything clear[1]?
都清楚了嗎？

→ Does anyone have any questions?
還有人有任何問題嗎？

→ Does everyone agree with[2] this?
每一個人都同意這一點嗎？

→ Is there anything I can clarify[3]?
還有其他我可以澄清的嗎？

→ Shall I go over the main points?
需要我確認一次重點嗎？

→ Any final questions?
還有任何最後的問題嗎？

→ Are we agreed[4]?
大家同意嗎？

會議 Conference

精選句型

Do you understand everything?

你們都明白嗎？

句型

understand + 名詞 / wh-子句 / how 子句

※ wh=who/what/where/when/which

句型範例

♣ Do you understand the points?
你瞭解重點嗎？

♣ Do you understand where to go?
你瞭解要去哪裡嗎？

Word Bank

1.clear   a. 清楚的

2.agree with~ 同意~

3.clarify   v. 澄清

4.agreed   a. 意見一致的

MP3 125

Unit 21

宣佈散會

精選例句

→ We'll stop[1] here for today.
今天就到這裡結束。

→ Let's finish here.
今天就到這裡結束。

→ Let's call it a day[2].
今天就到這裡結束。

→ Let's bring this to a close for today.
今天的會議就到此結束。

→ If there are no other comments, the meeting is finished.
假如沒有其他意見，會議結束了。

→ If there are no further points, we can finish here.
如果沒有進一步的重點，我們今天就到這裡結束。

→ I declare the meeting adjourned[3].
我宣佈散會。

會議 Conference

I declare the meeting adjourned.

我宣佈散會。

句型

declared +	受詞 + 形容詞
	that 子句

句型範例

❖ The accused man declared himself innocent.
被告聲稱他是無罪的。

❖ She declared that she didn't do it.
她宣稱這不是她做的。

Word Bank

1.stop　v. 結束

2.call it a day　今天到此結束

3.adjourn　v. 休會

單字整理

MP3 12

conference 會議

meeting 會議

meet 見面

discuss 討論

guess 猜測

begin 開始

start 開始

opportunity 機會

get down to 開始認真對待

keep the minutes 記錄會議

take notes 紀錄

report 報告

agenda 議程

item 項目

a copy of 一份

receive 收到

preview 預覽

in order 按順序

each 每一個

last 持續

finish 結束

會議 Conference

take 花費

spend 花費

aim 致力

improve 改進

agreement 同意

progress 進行

go over 重溫

last 上一次的

final 最後的

brainstorm 集思廣益

attention 注意

elaborate 詳盡闡述

comment 建議

appreciate 感激

add 補充

comment 發表意見

explain 解釋

say 說話

according to 根據

interrupt 打斷(講話或講話人)

單字整理

clarification 澄清

break 休息

intermission 中斷、暫停

resume 繼續

instead 作為替代

enough 足夠的

summarize 總結

sum up 總而言之

in brief 總而言之

簡報
Briefing

MP3 127

Unit
1

歡迎詞

精選例句

➔ Welcome, ladies and gentlemen.
各位先生、女士,歡迎。

➔ Good morning, gentlemen.
各位先生,早安。

➔ Good afternoon, everyone.
各位,午安。

➔ Thank you for coming.
謝謝各位出席。

➔ Are you ready?
你們準備好了嗎?

➔ Is everyone here?
大家都到齊了嗎?

➔ Please have a seat[1], ladies.
各位女士,請坐。

➔ I'm glad to see everyone is here.
很高興在此看到各位。

簡報 Briefing

精選句型

Please have a seat, ladies.

各位女士，請坐。

句型範例

✤ Have a seat, please.
請坐！

✤ Sit down, please.
請坐！

✤ Sit!
坐！

Word Bank

1.have a seat 請坐

128

Unit 2

開場白

精選例句

→ I'm going to talk about our CSR projects.
  我是要來談論有關我們的客服計畫。

→ The purpose of my presentation[1] is to introduce our annual projects.
  我今天簡報的目的，是要介紹我們的年度計畫。

→ I'm eager to show you my ideas.
  我迫不亟待要給各位看我的想法。

→ Today is a good opportunity[2] to accomplish[3] my purpose.
  今天是完成我的目的的好機會。

→ I'd like you to see what we have worked on for the last three months.
  我要各位瞧瞧我們過去三個月努力的結果。

→ I'm here to represent[4] our annual plans.
  我今天要報告的是我們的年度計畫。

簡報　Briefing

精選句型

I'm eager to ~

我迫不及待~

句 型

be 動詞 + eager to + 原形動詞

句型範例

❖ I am eager to see you.
　我迫不及待要見你！

❖ She is eager to read this book.
　她迫不及待要讀這本書。

❖ We are eager to learn more.
　我們迫不及待要多加學習。

Word Bank

1. presentation　n. 簡報

2. opportunity　n. 機會

3. accomplish　v. 完成

4. represent　v. 做報告

129

Unit 3

敬稱

精選例句

→ Mr. Chairman[1], ladies and gentlemen.
（男）主席、各位先生、女士。

→ Madam Chairman[2], ladies and gentlemen.
（女）主席、各位先生、女士。

→ Dr. Smith, ladies.
史密斯博士、各位女士。

→ Dr. Smith, Dr. Jones and gentlemen.
史密斯博士、瓊斯博士、各位先生。

→ Professor Smith, ladies and gentlemen.
史密斯教授、各位先生、女士。

→ Mr. Chairman, American hosts[3], ladies and gentlemen.
主席、美方主辦人、各位先生、女士。

→ Mr. Chairman, colleagues[4], ladies and gentlemen.
主席、各位同事、各位先生、女士。

簡報 Briefing

精選句型

Mr. Chairman, ladies and gentlemen.

(男)主席、各位先生、女士。

句型範例

* Ladies and gentlemen!
  各位先生、女士。

* Ladies!
  各位女士。

* Gentlemen!
  各位先生！

* Girls and boys.
  各位女孩、男孩！

Word Bank

1. Mr. Chairman （男）主席

2. Madam Chairman （女）主席

3. host n. 主人

4. colleague n. 同事

MP3 130

Unit 4

使用幻燈片

精選例句

→ Slide[1], please.
請放幻燈片。

→ Let's see the first slide.
我們來看第一張幻燈片。

→ Turn off[2] the light, please.
請關燈。

→ In the next slide, you'll see ~
在下一張幻燈片，你將會看到~

→ This slide shows that ~
這張幻燈片顯示出~

→ Sorry, the slide is upside down[3].
抱歉，幻燈片上下顛倒了。

→ Sorry, the slide is back to front[4].
抱歉，幻燈片前後相反了。

→ Can we get a better focus[5], please?
請調整一下焦距好嗎？

簡報 Briefing

精選句型

Turn off the light.

關燈。

句 型

turn + on(打開)
off(關掉)

※適用於電燈、瓦斯、音響設備的開關

句型範例

- ✤ Please turn on the light.
  請開燈。

- ✤ Turn off the radio.
  關掉收音機。

- ✤ Turn off the gas.
  關掉瓦斯。

Word Bank

1.slide n. 幻燈片
2.turn off v. 關（電器）
3.be upside down 上下顛倒
4.be back to front 前後相反
5.focus n. 焦距

MP3 131

Unit
5

簡報架構

精選例句

→ I'll begin by the latest[1] sales report.
我將從最新的銷售報告開始。

→ I'll start by describing the current[2]
position in Europe.
我將從説明目前在歐洲的定位開始。

→ Then I'll mention[3] some of the problems
we've encountered[4].
然後我會提及一些我們面臨的問題。

→ After that I'll consider the possibilities for
further growth[5] next year.
之後我會考慮明年成長得可能性。

→ Finally, I'll summarize my presentation.
最後我會總結我的簡報。

→ Before concluding with some
recommendations, I need to know your
ideas.
總結一些建議之前，我需要知道你們的想
法。

簡報 Briefing

精選句型

Before concluding ~

在總結之前，~

句型

before +
| 名詞 |
| 動詞 ing |
| 子句 |

句型範例

❖ We may die before tomorrow.
我們可能明天就會死。

❖ Ask your boss before making a purchase.
下單購買之前先問問你的老闆。

❖ Before you buy it, ask your mother.
買之前先問你母親。

Word Bank

1. latest　a. 最新的

2. current　a. 目前的

3. mention　v. 提及

4. encounter　v. 遭遇

5. growth　n. 成長

MP3 132

Unit
6

簡報主題

精選例句

→ The whole point of my representation is about profit.
我的簡報的宗旨就是有關利潤。

→ The goal for this presentation is to ensure you a good environment[1].
這次簡報的宗旨是要確保你們一個好的環境。

→ Then I'll move on to some of the achievements[2] we've made in Asia.
然後我會進行到我們在亞洲的一些成就。

→ After that I'll show you our opportunities in Africa.
之後,我會給各位看我們在非洲的機會。

→ Lastly, I'll quickly recap[3] before concluding with some recommendations[4].
最後,下結論之前,我會快速地總結之前的簡報。

→ Let's turn now to Asia.
現在我們開始進行亞洲的報告。

→ I'll show you how we overcame[5] them.
我要向各位展示我們如何克服他們。

簡報 **Briefing**

精選句型

I'll show you how ~

我要向各位展示如何~

句 型

show you + | 名詞 / wh-子句 / how 子句 |

※ wh=who/what/where/when/which

句型範例

✤ I'll show you something.
  我要展示一些東西給你看。

✤ I'll show you how we operate it.
  我要展示我們如何操作。

Word Bank

1.environment n. 環境

2.achievement n. 成就

3.recap v. 重述要點

4.recommendation n. 建議

5.overcome v. 克服

MP3 133

Unit 7
強調論點

精選例句

→ What I am saying is ~
  我說的是~

→ I suggest we follow[1] the rules.
  我建議我們依這個規則。

→ I suggest we take item 2 last.
  我建議我們最後再討論議程二。

→ To sum up[2], I'll offer[3] this position[4] to him.
  總而言之,我將會提供這個職位給他。

→ I emphasize[5] the importance of this plan.
  我強調這個計畫的重要性。

→ I advocate[6] reforming the CSR system.
  我主張改良客服系統。

→ I believe that we have to accomplish this mission.
  我相信我們應該完成這個任務。

簡報 Briefing

 精選句型

What I am saying is ~

我說的是~

句 型

What I + | be 動詞 / 一般動詞 | + is ~

句型範例

❖ What I am saying is true and reasonable.
  我所說的是事實且有理的。

❖ What I meant is over 85%.
  我的意思是超過百分之八十五。

Word Bank

1. follow v. 跟隨
2. sum up 總而言之
3. offer v. 提供
4. position n. 職位
5. emphasize v. 強調
6. advocate v. 主張

MP3 134

Unit
8

條列式說明

精選例句

→ There are four points.
有四個重點。

→ I'll show you one by one[1].
我會一個一個展示給各位看。

→ Firstly~, secondly~, thirdly~, lastly~
首先~，再來是~，第三~，最後~

→ First of all, I'll show you our proposal[2].
首先，我會展示給各位我們的計畫。

→ Then you will see lots of layouts[3].
然後你們會看見很多的版型。

→ After that, we supply[4] you with books and magazines.
在這個之後，我們會提供給各位書籍和雜誌。

→ Finally, we need to make sure which one is better.
最後，我們需要確定那一個比較好。

簡報 **Briefing**

精選句型

show you one by one
一個一個展示給你

句型

one by one 一個接一個
day by day 一天又一天

句型範例

✤ One by one the lights went out.
燈一個個地熄了。

✤ He is getting worse day by day.
他一天比一天糟糕。

Word Bank

1. one by one 一個接著一個

2. proposal　n. 計畫

3. layout　n. 版型

4. supply　n. 提供

Unit
9

詳細說明

 精選例句

→ I'd like to deal with[1] it now.
我現在要來處理。

→ Let me explain it to you in greater detail.
讓我跟各位解說更詳細的細節。

→ Now, let's talk about this part.
讓我們現在討論這個部分。

→ I'd like to enter into[2] some details on this part.
針對這個部分我將討論更多細節。

→ I'd like to spend more time describing[3] it in detail.
我會花更多時間來說明它的細節。

→ I'll show you all the details now.
現在我會給各位看更多細節。

→ We'll discuss this part in detail as we go on[4] later.
等一下進行到這裡時,我們會再來討論。

簡報 **Briefing**

(精選句型)

I'd like to spend more time.

我會花更多時間。

句 型

spend + 時間 / 錢 / 精力

句型範例

* I spent $100 on the bike.
  我花了一百美元買下那輛自行車。

* They spent 2 months touring Europe.
  他們花了二個月時間周遊歐洲。

Word Bank

1.deal with 處理

2.enter into 討論

3.describe 描述

4.go on 進行

Unit 10
簡化說明

 精選例句

→ I don't have time to go into detail on this part.
這個部分我沒有時間討論細節。

→ I have to skip many details of this part.
這個部分我必須省略許多細節。

→ My time is running short[1], so I'll be brief[2].
我的時間不夠了,所以我會簡單帶過。

→ Let me merely[3] say that ~
我只是要說,~

→ I'll review this part succinctly[4].
我來簡單地回顧這個部分。

→ I'm not going to spend too much time on it.
我不打算花太多時間在這上面。

→ I'll go through the next point briefly[5].
我會簡單地討論下個重點。

簡報 **Briefing**

精選句型

My time is running short.
我的時間不夠了。

句型

run +
short
out

句型範例

❖ My pocket money is running short.
我經濟拮据。

❖ The sugar is running short.
沒有砂糖了。

❖ Our food soon ran out.
我們的食物不久就吃光了。

Word Bank

1. be running short 不夠
2. brief   n. 簡報
3. merely   adv. 只是
4. succinctly   adv. 簡潔地
5. briefly   adv. 簡短地

提供發問

→ Do feel free to interrupt[1] me if you have any questions.
如果有任何問題，請盡量發問。

→ I'll try to answer all of your questions after the presentation[2].
我會試著在簡報之後回答你們的所有問題。

→ Now I'll try to answer any questions you may have.
現在我會試著回答任何你們提出的問題。

→ Are there any questions?
還有任何問題嗎？

→ Do you have any questions?
你們還有任何問題嗎？

→ Are there any final[3] questions?
最後還有問題嗎？

簡報 **Briefing**

精選句型

Do feel free to ~

請不要客氣,盡量~

句型

do feel free to + 原形動詞

句型範例

✤ Please do feel free to contact us.
請不要客氣聯絡我們。

✤ Do feel free to visit us.
請隨時拜訪我們。

Word Bank

1.interrupt v. 干擾

2.presentation n. 簡報

3.final a. 最後的

Unit 12

提供資料

精選例句

→ Please turn to page 11.
請翻到第十一頁。

→ I want you to see the data[1] we have.
我要各位看看我們有的數據。

→ The forecasts[2] show that we would lose our orders.
預測顯示出我們將會失去訂單。

→ Each number on the chart[3] represents a result.
曲線圖上的每一個數字代表一個結果。

→ As you can see, here is our solution[4].
就各位所看到的,這是我們的解決方法。

→ Most of our clients don't like our products.
大部分我們的客戶不喜歡我們的產品。

(精選句型)

Most of our clients don't like it.

大部分我們的客戶不喜歡它。

句型

Most of + | 可數複數名詞
子句
不可數名詞 | + 複數動詞

句型範例

❖ Most of them don't agree with his opinion.
他們之中大多數人都不同意他的意見。

❖ Most of the time, we did nothing.
大部分時間我們無所事事。

Word Bank

1.data　n. 數據

2.forecast　n. 預測

3.chart　n. 圖表

4.solution　n. 解決的方法

139

說明研究報告

精選例句

→ I've told you about the spring sales plans.
我已經告訴您有關春季銷售計畫了。

→ That's all I siad about the sales plans.
這就是我提過的銷售計畫。

→ We've looked at his studies[1].
我們已經看過他的研究了。

→ Now we'll move on to No. 3.
現在我們進行到第三點。

→ Next is about the CSR system[2].
下一項是有關客服系統。

→ I'd like to discuss the new design.
我想要來討論新的設計。

→ Let's look at the whiteboard[3].
我們來看看白板。

→ What does SOP mean[4]?
SOP 是什麼意思？

簡報 **Briefing**

精選句型

Let's look at the whiteboard.

我們來看看白板。

句 型

· look at 看、查看
· look after 照料
· look ahead 考慮到將來
· look into 查資料

句 型 範 例

✤ I have to look after my brother tonight.
我今晚必須照顧我弟弟。

Word Bank

1.study   n. 研究報告

2.system   n. 系統

3.whiteboard   n. 白板

4.mean   v. 意義

Unit
14
停止討論

精選例句

➤ I'll leave out[1] this unit.
我先不管這個單元。

➤ I have to skip[2] this one now.
我現在必須跳過這個。

➤ I have to skip this question due to the time limitation[3].
因為時間限制，我必須跳過這個問題。

➤ Sorry, I have to skip Chapter 5.
抱歉，我必須跳過第五章。

➤ I have to skip from unit 5 to unit 6.
我必須省略第五章直接跳到第六章。

➤ We shall discuss during the Q&A period[4].
在問與答階段我們再來討論。

➤ Because of the time, I won't show you this in detail.
因為時間，我將不會展示細節給各位。

簡報 **Briefing**

Because of the time, ~

因為時間的因素，~

句 型

because + | of + 名詞 |
| 子句 |

句型範例

❖ We didn't go to school because of the storm.
因為暴風雨，我們不用去上學。

❖ Because your mistake, I lost my job.
因為你的錯誤，我失去工作。

Word Bank

1.leave out 不考慮

2.skip v. 跳過不做

3.limitation n. 限制

4.period n. 階段

MP3 141

Unit 15
稍後補充說明

精選例句

→ I'll have more to show you that in a few minutes[1].
等一下我將會給各位看更多東西。

→ I'll show you more details later.
稍後我將會展示更多細節。

→ I'll tell you about it in detail.
我將會告訴各位更多細節。

→ I'll refer[2] to this part later.
稍後我會談論到這個部分。

→ We'll return[3] to it later.
我們稍後再回來（這個主題）。

→ I'll give you some examples later.
稍後我會給各位一些範例。

→ If we have time, I'll return to this point.
如果我們有時間,我會回到這個主題。

→ Maybe we'll go through it later.
也許我們稍後會談論到。

簡報 **Briefing**

精選句型

I'll give you some examples later.

稍後我會給各位一些範例。

句 型

主詞 + 未來式助動詞 ~+ later

※ later 表名詞（之後）或形容詞（之後的）

句型範例

❖ We'll discuss this in a later chapter.
我們將在稍後的一章中對這個作探討。

❖ I'll tell you later.
我以後再告訴你。

Word Bank

1.in a few minutes 即將

2.refer v. 論及

3.return v. 回歸

Unit
16

細節說明

精選例句

→ I'll show you all the details.
我會展示給各位看所有的細節。

→ I'd like to deal with this question later.
我想要稍後再處理這個問題。

→ I'll come back to this question later in my talk on annual sales plans.
等論及年度銷售計畫時,再回到這個問題上。

→ I won't comment[1] on this now.
我現在不想發表評論。

→ How do we make BCQ Company place an order[2] soon?
如何讓 BCQ 公司儘速下訂單?

→ We will solve[3] every problem we encounter, right?
我們會解決每一個我們所遭遇的問題,對吧?

→ I'll explain how the machine operates[4].
我會解釋這部機器如何運作。

How do we make ~?

我們如何讓~？

句 型

How + to + 原形動詞

助動詞 + S

句型範例

* How to make her happy?
  如何讓她快樂？

* How should I operate it?
  我要如何操作？

* How should I get there?
  如何到那裡？

Word Bank

1.comment v. 發表評論

2.place an order 下訂單

3.solve v. 解決

4.operate v. 運作

143

支持論點

精選例句

→ I'm in favor of[1] the annual plans.
我同意年度計畫。

→ We favor[2] Mr. Smith's plan.
我們贊成史密斯先生的計劃。

→ I agree[3] with you.
我同意你。

→ I agree with Mr. Smith on this point.
在這個論點上，我同意史密斯先生。

→ I come out in favor of[4] what Mr. Smith is proposing,
我支持史密斯先生的提案。

→ I'd like to support[5] his opinion.
我將支持他的論點。

→ I back him up[6].
我支持他。

簡報 **Briefing**

I'm in favor of it.

我同意這件事。

句 型

be + in favor of + | 名詞 / 動詞 ing |

句型範例

✤ I'm in favor of your decision.
我同意你的決定。

✤ I am in favor of moving out.
我同意搬出去。

Word Bank

1. in favor of 同意
2. favor v. 同意
3. agree v. 同意
4. come out in favor of 支持
5. support v. 支持
6. back up 支持

MP3 144

Unit 18

反對論點

精選例句

→ I don't think so.
我不這麼認為。

→ I don't agree with you on many things.
我和你在許多事情上意見不一致。

→ We oppose[1] the idea at all.
我們絲毫不贊成這個想法。

→ I'm opposed to working with others.
我反對與他人一起工作。

→ I'm against[2] using death as a punishment.
我反對將死刑當成一種懲罰方式。

→ I object[3] to the plan.
我反對這項計畫。

→ I disputed[4] the election results.
我質疑選舉結果。

精選句型

We oppose the idea at all.
我們絲毫不贊成這個想法。

句 型

| 否定句 | + at all (根本) |

| 問句
條件句
肯定句 | + at all (究竟) |

句型範例

✤ I don't like her at all.
我一點都不喜歡她。

✤ He'll come before 12 if he comes at all.
如果他真的要來的話,肯定在十二點以前。

Word Bank

1.oppose　v. 反對

2.be against　反對

3.object　v. 反對

4.dispute　v. 質疑

Unit
19

提出建議

➤ Here is my advice.
以下是我的建議。

➤ My recommendations are in two parts.
我的建議有兩大部分。

➤ I propose[1] the following strategy[2].
我提出以下的策略。

➤ I suggest we visit Taipei.
我建議我們去臺北參觀。

➤ We offered him the computer for US $100.
這電腦我們向他開價一百美元。

➤ My solution to this problem is a refund[3].
我對這個問題的解決方法是退費。

➤ I'll remind you of the main points we've considered.
我會提醒您我們已經考慮過的重點。

I'll remind you of ~

我會提醒您~

句 型

remind someone of + something

句型範例

❖ This hotel reminds me of the one in Taipei.
這家旅館使我想起台北的那一家。

❖ You remind me of my father.
你讓我想起我父親。

Word Bank

1. propose   v. 提議

2. strategy   n. 策略

3. refund   n. 退費

簡報總結

精選例句

→ I'd like to sum up now.
現在我要總結。

→ Let's sum up now, shall we?
讓我們來下結論好嗎?

→ Let's summarize briefly[1] what we've looked at.
我們簡短地總結一下我們看過的事項。

→ I'd like to conclude with a picture.
我要用一張圖片作結論。

→ To conclude, BCQ Company promise[2] to sell two million cars.
總結是,BCQ 公司答應賣出兩百萬輛車。

→ To summarize my points, you are the decision maker[3].
總結我的論點,你是做決定者。

→ In conclusion, I'll do everything to satisfy[4] our customers.
結論是,我將盡一切努力令我們的顧客滿意。

精選句型

To conclude, ~

總結是~

句 型

To + 原形動詞 , + 主詞 + 動詞

句 型 範 例

❖ To be honest, I have nothing to say.
老實說,我沒什麼好說的。

❖ To tell you the truth, I'm pretty worried,
告訴你實話,我很擔心。

3
1
7

Word Bank

1.briefly   adv. 簡短地

2.promise   v. 答應

3.decision maker 做決定者

4.satisfy   v. 滿足

MP3 147

Unit
21

結束簡報

精選例句

→ Thank you, gentlemen.
感謝各位。

→ Thank you for being here today.
感謝各位今天的出席。

→ Thank you for your time.
感謝各位撥冗。

→ Thank you for your patience[1].
感謝各位的耐心（聽完簡報）。

→ Thank you for your attention[2].
感謝各位的專心（聽完簡報）。

→ Finally, let me remind you of some of the issues[3].
最後，我提醒你們一些事項。

→ If you still have questions, please let me know.
如果你們還有問題，請讓我知道。

簡報 **Briefing**

精選句型

Finally, ~

最後，~

句型

- Firstly, ~ 首先，~
- Secondly, ~ 再來，~
- Thirdly, ~ 第三，~
- Finally, ~ 最後，~

句型範例

❖ Firstly, let us deal with the most important issue.
首先讓我們來處理最緊要的問題。

❖ Secondly, you give him a call.
第二，你打電話給他。

❖ Finally, I'd meet you at the airport.
最後，我會去機場接機。

Word Bank

1. patience   n. 耐心

2. attention   n. 注意力

3. issue n. 議題

單字整理

MP3 14?

briefing 簡報

slide 幻燈片

first 第一

second 第二

then 然後

after that 之後

before that 之前

next 下一個

finally 最後

talk about 談論

title 主題

talk 談論

announce 宣布

issue 問題

introduce 介紹

mean 表示

stand for 代表

indicate 表示

prove 證明

highlight 凸顯

clarify 澄清

progress 進步

carry on 繼續

purpose 目的

project 計畫

aim 目標

layout 大綱

presentation 呈現

present 表現

overview 概觀

detail 細節

adjourn 休會

look at 看

issue 問題

content 內容

figure 圖表

chart 曲線圖

design 設計

policy 策略

advertisement 廣告

service 服務

單字整理

creative 創造性的

idea 點子

clear 清楚的

agree with 同意

agreed 意見一致的

be held 被舉行

stop 結束

break 休息

call it a day 今天到此結束

Chapter
8

商展
Trade Show

Unit 1

攤位佈置

精選例句

→ We need to design our booth[1].
我們必須要設計自己的攤位。

→ How should I set up our booth display[2]?
我應該如何佈置我們的攤位展示?

→ We tried to make our booth stand out[3].
我們試著要將我們的攤位凸顯。

→ Where should I post[4] this poster[5]?
我應該將這張海報貼在哪裡?

→ Where can I have the display table?
哪裡有展示桌?

→ Where can I take the map of exhibition hall?
我可以在哪裡拿到會場佈置圖?

→ Are there any electrical outlets available?
有沒有插座?

→ We have to establish our show space.
我們必需要建立我們的展示空間。

商展 Trade Show

精選句型

make ~ stand out

要將~凸顯

句 型

make something + 形容詞

句型範例

✤ We tried to make it different.
  我們試著讓它不同。

✤ They always make things special.
  他們總會令事情顯得特別。

Word Bank

1. booth   n. 攤位
2. display   n. 展示
3. stand out   凸顯
4. post   v. 張貼
5. poster   n. 海報

MP3 150

Unit 2

自我介紹

精選例句

✈ How can I help you?
需要我協助嗎？

✈ Hi, I'm David Jones.
嗨，我是大衛・瓊斯。

✈ This is my business card.
這是我的名片。

✈ Let me introduce¹ myself.
讓我自我介紹。

✈ David Jones. Nice to meet you.
（我是）大衛・瓊斯。很高興認識你。

✈ I'm David Jones of BCQ Company.
我是 BCQ 公司的大衛・瓊斯。

✈ I'm the salesman² of BCQ Company.
我是 BCQ 公司的業務。

✈ I'm general manager³ of BCQ Company.
我是 BCQ 公司的總經理。

商展 Trade Show

精選句型

How can I help you?

需要我協助嗎？

句型範例

✤ May I help you?
   需要我協助嗎？

✤ How may I help you?
   需要我協助嗎？

✤ Do you need help?
   你需要幫助嗎？

✤ What can I do for you?
   我可以為你做什麼嗎？

Word Bank

1. introduce   v. 介紹

2. salesman   n. 業務人員

3. general manager 總經理

Unit 3

介紹公司

→ We sell keyboards.
我們賣鍵盤。

→ We are a sports equipment[1] company.
我們是一家運動器材公司。

→ We often do business[2] with Japanese.
我們常跟日本人做生意。

→ My company is an Internet company based in Taiwan.
我的公司是一家在台灣的網路公司。

→ Have you ever heard of BCQ?
您聽過 BCQ 嗎?

→ BCQ is a subsidiary company of Intel.
BCQ 是英特爾公司的子公司。

→ We are one of the subsidiary companies[3] of IBM.
我們是 IBM 公司的其中一家子公司。

商展 Trade Show

精選句型

Have you ever heard of ~?

您曾經聽過~嗎？

句型

Have you ever + 動詞過去分詞

※適用於疑問句

句型範例

✦ Have you ever heard of this book?
你聽過這本書嗎？

✦ Have you ever done it?
你做過這件事嗎？

Word Bank

1. equipment　n. 設備

2. do business　從事生意

3. subsidiary company 子公司

MP3 152

參展術語

精選例句

→ Let me show[1] you.
我展示給您看。

→ Let me show you something special.
我展示給您看一些特別的東西。

→ Would you like to take a look[2]?
您要看一看嗎？

→ I see you're looking at this.
我看到您正在注意這個。

→ Are you interested in our products?
你對我們的產品感興趣嗎？

→ Do you want to try it?
您要試一試嗎？

→ What are you interested in?
你對什麼（產品）感興趣？

→ Let me explain this to you.
我來解釋給您聽。

商展 Trade Show

精選句型

What are you interested in?

你對什麼（產品）感興趣？

句型

be interested in + 名詞(人/事/物)

句型範例

* I am interested in your computers.
  我對你們的電腦有興趣。

* We are interested in Mary.
  我們對瑪莉有興趣。

Word Bank

1.show v. 展示

2.take a look 看一眼

Unit 5

介紹商品

精選例句

→ Do you want to know about our products?
您想瞭解一下我們的產品嗎？

→ We have several[1] kinds of keyboards.
我們有許多種鍵盤。

→ Our best selling[2] keyboard is this one.
我們賣得最好的鍵盤是這一個。

→ This set[3] includes a table and four chairs.
這一整組包括一張桌子和四張椅子。

→ This chair is made of wood.
這張椅子是木頭製的。

→ It is two feet high[4].
這個有兩呎高。

→ It is one kilogram in weight[5].
它有一公斤重。

商展 **Trade Show**

精選句型

This chair is made of wood.

這張椅子是木頭製的。

句 型

| be + | made of + 名詞（材質未變） |
| | made from + 名詞（材質改變） |

句型範例

* This table is made of wood.
  這張桌子是木頭製的。

* The wine is made from grapes.
  這酒是用葡萄釀製的。

Word Bank

1. several   a. 幾個的
2. best selling   熱銷
3. set   n. 組
4. high   n. 高度
5. weight   n. 重量

商品的優勢

→ You'll find our prices very favorable[1].
你會發現我們的價格非常優惠。

→ I'm sure you'll find our price worth[2] accepting[3].
我相信你會認為我方的價格值得接受。

→ I'll try my best to meet your requirements[4].
我會盡量滿足你們的需求。

→ Our prices are most attractive[5].
你會發現我方的價格極有競爭力。

→ Our product is lower priced than the competition[6].
我們產品價格比同行競爭者低廉。

→ Our product is competitive on the international market.
我們的產品在國際市場上具有競爭力。

商展 Trade Show ✈

精選句型

I'll try my best to ~

我會盡量~

句 型

try someone's best to + 原形動詞

句型範例

❖ I'll try my best to teach him.
我會盡量去教他。

❖ Try your best.
盡你所能。

Word Bank

1. favorable　a. 適合的
2. worth　a. 有價值
3. accept　v. 接受
4. meet your requirement
符合你的需求
5. attractive　a. 具吸引力的
6. competition　n. 競爭

MP3 155

Unit
7

樣品

➤ It's free.
免費的。

➤ Help yourself.
請自取。

➤ Free gift.
免費贈品。

➤ We have some samples[1] in our showroom[2].
我們在展示間有一些樣本。

➤ Could you provide[3] some samples free of charge?
能否免費提供一些樣品?

➤ We can make a discount[4] on the samples.
我們有樣品可以打個折扣。

➤ They are not for sale.
它們是非賣品。

商展 **Trade Show**

精選句型

make a discount on ~

~打個折扣

句 型

make a discount on + something

句型範例

❖ Can you make a discount on it?
這個東西你可以打折嗎？

❖ You should make a discount on the total.
你應該全部打個折扣。

❖ Can you make a discount?
可以打折嗎？

Word Bank

1.sample　n. 樣品

2.showroom　n. 展示房間

3.provide　v. 提供

4.discount　n. 折扣

精選例句

→ I've brought a series[1] of catalogues on our samples with me.
我帶來了我們的樣本型錄。

→ Here are our price lists.
這是我們的價目單。

→ Here is our new catalogue. It's free.
這裡有我們新的型錄。是免費的

→ You'll find the required items, specifications[2] and quantities[3] all there.
你可以在上面知道所需的品種、規格和數量。

→ May I have a catalogue covering your products?
能否給我一份你們所有商品的型錄？

→ May I have a copy of your catalogue?
可以給我一份你們的型錄嗎？

→ Do you have a catalogue of that item?
有那個品項的型錄嗎？

商展 **Trade Show**

(精選句型)

I've brought ~

我帶來了~

句型

| I/You/They/we + have | + 動詞過去分詞 |
| He/She/David + has | |

句型範例

❖ I have seen it.
我已經看過了。

❖ She has finished it on time.
她已經準時完成了。

3
3
9

Word Bank

1. series   n. 套、輯

2. specification   n. 詳述

3. quantity   n. 數量

MP3 157

Unit 9

詢價

精選例句

→ Could you give us some idea about your price?
你能向我們介紹一下價格嗎?

→ I'd like to have your lowest quotations[1], CIF Taipei.
我想請你們報臺北的最低價。

→ Would you please make your prices CIF including five percent[2]?
能請你報包括百分之五傭金在內的到岸價嗎?

→ Would you give me an offer for Item No. 5?
你能給我第五號商品的報價嗎?

→ May I have your offer of Model 703?
可以給我 703 型號商品的報價嗎?

→ Are all your quotations CIF?
你們所有的報盤都是到岸價嗎?

→ We can make them FOB if you like.
如果你要離岸價的話,我們可以報。

商展 Trade Show

精選句型

~ if you like

如果你要的話，~

句型

主詞 + 動詞 + if you like

句型範例

❖ We'll be there on time if you like.

如果你要，我們會準時到達。

❖ I can call him if you like.

如果你要，我會打電話給他。

Word Bank

1.quotation n. 報價

2.percent n. 百分比

Unit 10

報價

➔ Here is our latest price sheet.
這是我們最新的報價單。

➔ All the prices in the lists are subject to[1] our confirmation[2].
表上的價格以我方最後確認為準。

➔ Our prices are on a CIF basis.
我的報價都是成本加運費保險的到岸價格。

➔ Do you quote[3] FOB or CIF?
你們是報離岸價還是到岸價？

➔ The offer is subject to immediate[4] acceptance[5].
這個價格要立即接受才有效。

➔ How long will you keep your offer valid[6]?
報價的有效期多長？

➔ It will remain firm till Friday.
有效期到星期五為止。

商展 **Trade Show**

精選句型

Do you ~?
你(們)是~？

句型

| Do you/they/I | + 原形動詞 |
| Does he/she/David | |

句型範例

✤ Do they like it?
　他們喜歡它嗎？

✤ Do you really think so?
　你真的這樣認為？

✤ Does she live in Taipei?
　她住在台北嗎？

Word Bank

1. be subject to 以~為條件的
2. confirmation n. 確認
3. quote v. 報價
4. immediate a. 立即的
5. acceptance n. 接受
6. valid a. 有效的

159

精選例句

→ It's too expensive[1].
太貴了!

→ No discount?
沒有折扣?

→ Could you give us some discount?
你能給我們一些折扣嗎?

→ What if my quantity[2] is large?
如果我訂購的數量相當大呢?

→ How about a ten percent discount?
你覺得百分之十的折扣呢?

→ Could you give us some discount if my
quantity is large[3]?
如果我訂購的數量相當大,你能給我們一些
折扣呢?

→ I hope you'll quote us on your best terms.
我希望你能按最優惠條件報價。

商展

(精選句型)

What if my quantity is large?

如果我訂購的數量相當大呢？

句 型

What if + 主詞 + 一般動詞

句型範例

* What if you are wrong?
  如果你錯了呢？

* What if he is not your best man?
  如果他不是你最佳人選呢？

Word Bank

1. expensive　a. 昂貴的

2. quantity　n. 數量

3. large　a. 大的

Unit
12

交貨

精選例句

→ How long does it usually take to make delivery[1]?
通常要多長的時間才可以交貨？

→ You have to deliver all goods by September 3.
你們必須在九月三號前交貨。

→ How do you deliver our products?
你們如何運送我們的商品？

→ We guarantee[2] prompt[3] delivery of goods.
我們保證立即交貨。

→ We will make delivery on time.
我們會準時交貨。

→ The goods will be transported to Taipei by air.
貨物將用空運送到臺北。

→ I'll send your goods by sea.
我會用海運運送你的商品。

商展 **Trade Show**

精選句型

I'll send your goods by sea.

我會用海運運送你的商品。

句型

by +
sea(海運)
air(空運)

句型範例

❖ We'll deliver it by air.
我們會用空運運送。

❖ Could you send it to me by sea?
你可以用海運寄送給我嗎？

Word Bank

1. delivery v. 運送

2. guarantee v. 保證

3. prompt a. 迅速的

Unit
13

庫存量

➔ What about the supply[1] position[2]?
　供應情況怎樣？

➔ Do you think you will get any more in a
　short time?
　你們最近還會進貨嗎？

➔ When will you get ready for new
　supply?
　什麼時候你們會有新貨供應？

➔ For most of the articles[3] in the catalogue,
　we have good supply.
　目錄中大部分的貨源都很充足。

➔ Our old stock[4] has been entirely cleared
　out[5].
　我們舊的存貨已全部出清。

➔ We're sorry nothing is available now.
　很遺憾，目前無貨可以供應。

商展 Trade Show

精選句型

Do you think~?

你認為～嗎？

句 型

Do you think + 主詞 + 一般動詞

句型範例

✤ Do you thing you can overcome it?
你覺得你可以克服嗎？

✤ Do you think we can make it?
你覺得我們可以辦得到嗎？

✤ Do you really think it's possible?
你真的覺得有可能嗎？

Word Bank

1. supply v. 提供
2. position n. 現況
3. article n. 商品
4. stock n. 庫存
5. cleared out 出空

162

Unit 14

對商品的評價

精選例句

→ Pretty attractive[1] to us.
對我們很有吸引力。

→ It sounds good.
聽起來不錯。

→ They look very good.
他們看起來不錯！

→ I'm interested in No.3 and No. 4.
我對三號和四號感興趣。

→ I'm interested in your hardware[2].
我對你們的硬體感興趣。

→ This is the one we're interested in.
我們對這一種比較感興趣。

→ If your prices are good, I can place an order right now[3].
如果你們的價格合理，我可以馬上訂貨。

→ What's the size of this product?
這個產品的尺寸是多少？

商展 Trade Show

精選句型

It sounds good.

聽起來不錯。

句型

It sounds + 形容詞

句型範例

✤ It sounds great.
聽起來很好。

✤ It sounds terrible.
聽起來很可怕。

✤ It sounds interesting.
聽起來很有趣。

Word Bank

1. attractive　a. 具吸引力的

2. hardware　n. 硬體

3. right now　就是現在

163

商品的需求

精選例句

→ What's your specifications[1]?
你們的規格是什麼？

→ I'm thinking about buying keyboards.
我想訂購鍵盤。

→ Would you accept orders according to[2]
our patterns[3]?
能否接受根據我們的樣式的訂貨？

→ All of our products meet your requirements[4].
所有我們的商品都符合你們的需要。

→ We are thinking about placing an order.
我們正在考慮訂貨。

→ I'd like to get some idea of your shoes.
我想瞭解一下有關你們鞋子的情況。

→ What kind of literature exactly?
到底你要什麼樣的資料？

精選句型

I'm thinking about ~

我想~

句 型

be thinking about + 動詞 ing

句型範例

✤ I'm thinking about telling him the truth.
我打算告訴他實話。

✤ I'm thinking about calling him.
我打算打電話給他。

✤ I am thinking about making some changes.
我想做一些改變。

Word Bank

1. specification   n. 詳述

2. according to   根據~

3. pattern   n. 樣本

4. requirement   n. 需求

數量的需求

→ How many pieces do you want?
你要多少數量？

→ It's an attractive quantity.
數量很大。

→ Running shoes are in high demand[1]
these days.
最近運動鞋的需求量很大，

→ I'll order 8,000 pieces.
我們會訂八千件。

→ Can I have your specific[2] inquiry[3]?
可否告知您的詳細需求？

→ Would you tell us what quantity you
need?
能否請你談談你的需求數量？

→ We need 100 sets[4] of that model[5].
那一款我們需要100套。

商展 Trade Show

精選句型

How many pieces ~?

多少~？

句 型

How many + 複數名詞

句型範例

❧ How many books have you read?
你讀過多少書？

❧ How many countries have you ever been to?
你曾經到過多少國家？

Word Bank

1. demand　v. 要求
2. specific　a. 特殊的
3. inquiry　n. 需求
4. set　n. 一套
5. model　n. 樣式

Unit
17

對市場的評價

精選例句

→ How is the fur market?
皮貨市場如何？

→ It's not very brisk[1].
並不太景氣。

→ The selling is getting better.
銷售越來越好。

→ You know the market has become very competitive[2].
你知道的，市場的競爭很激烈。

→ I think some of the items will find a ready market in Canada.
我覺得有些商品在加拿大會有銷路。

→ When the next supply[3] comes in, we'll let you know.
等下一批貨到貨時，我們就會讓你知道。

→ There's no market for these goods.
這些貨物沒有銷路。

精選句型

The selling is getting better.

銷售越來越好。

句型

be getting + 形容詞比較級

句型範例

* It's getting worse.
  越來越糟！
* It's getting hotter.
  越來越熱！
* It's getting harder to find clients.
  越來越難找到客戶。

Word Bank

1. brisk　a. 興旺的

2. competitive　a. 具競爭性的

3. supply　n. 供給

166

與客戶互動

精選例句

→ You should come over to booth 301.
你應該到301攤位來。

→ What do you think of our stuff[1]?
你覺得我們的東西如何？

→ We have plenty[2] of styles.
我們有很多種款式。

→ I guarantee you'll be satisfied with[3] our quality[4].
我保證你會滿意我們的品質。

→ Do you want to take a look?
你想要看一看嗎？

→ You may save 30 percent.
你可以省下三成。

→ It's too pity[5] if you don't buy them.
你如果不買就太可惜了。

→ It's your last chance for such good deal.
像這樣好的交易，是你最後的機會。

358

商展 **Trade Show**

精選句型

It's too pity if ~

如果~就太可惜了

句 型

be too + 形容詞 + if ~

句型範例

❖ It's too bad if you're not doing a good job.
如果你不好好表現就太糟糕了。

❖ It's too ridiculous if you think about it.
如果你這麼認為就太詭異了。

Word Bank

1. stuff　n. 東西
2. plenty　n. 很多
3. be satisfied with　對~滿意
4. quality　n. 品質
5. pity　a. 可惜的

推託用語

精選例句

➤ Let me figure it out[1].
讓我算一下。

➤ Let me put it this way.
讓我這麼說吧。

➤ I'll have to ask my boss first.
我必須先問一下我的老闆。

➤ There would be no problem, I suppose[2].
我想這毫無問題。

➤ I don't catch your question[3].
我沒聽清楚你的問題。

➤ Let me see what I can do.
我想想我能怎麼處理。

➤ Can you give me some feedback[4]?
你能給我一些回應嗎?

➤ I'll remember that.
我會記住。

I don't catch your question.

我沒聽清楚你的問題。

句型

catch +
| someone's 名詞 |
| what someone said |

※多用在否定或疑問句型

句型範例

✤ We didn't catch your question.
我們沒聽清楚你的問題。

✤ I didn't catch what the teacher said.
我沒有聽清楚老師説的話。

Word Bank

1.figure out 理解

2.suppose v. 推測

3.catch your question 聽得懂問題

4.feedback n. 回應

單字整理

MP3 168

trade show 商展

exhibition 展覽

booth 攤位

display 展示

booth 攤位

stand out 凸顯

post 張貼

poster 海報

showroom 展示房間

outlet 插座

establish 建立

set up 豎立

sell 銷售

show 表現

exhibit 展示

inquiry 需求

provide 提供

supply 供應

demand 要求

introduce 介紹

salesman 業務人員

商展　Trade Show

business card 名片
brochure 小冊子
leaflet 傳單
booklet 小冊子
specific 特殊的
equipment 設備
do business 從事生意
product 產品
sample 樣品
set 套組
size 尺寸
high 高度
weight 重量
color 顏色
favorable 適合的
worth 有價值
accept 接受
requirement 需求
attractive 具吸引力的
competition 競爭

單字整理

discount 折扣

catalogue 型錄

pattern 樣本

specification 詳述

quantity 數量

quality 品質

stock 庫存

cleared out 出空

selling season 銷售季節

出差英語一把罩

> 雅致風靡　典藏文化

親愛的顧客您好，感謝您購買這本書。即日起，填寫讀者回函卡寄回至本公司，我們每月將抽出一百名回函讀者，寄出精美禮物並享有生日當月購書優惠！想知道更多更即時的消息，歡迎加入"永續圖書粉絲團" 您也可以選擇傳真、掃描或用本公司準備的免郵回函寄回，謝謝。

傳真電話：（02）8647-3660　　　　電子信箱：yungjiuh@ms45.hinet.net

姓名：		性別：　□男　□女	
出生日期：　年　月　日		電話：	
學歷：		職業：	
E-mail：			
地址：□□□			
從何處購買此書：		購買金額：　　　元	
購買本書動機：□封面 □書名□排版 □內容 □作者 □偶然衝動			
你對本書的意見： 內容：□滿意□尚可□待改進　編輯：□滿意□尚可□待改進 封面：□滿意□尚可□待改進　定價：□滿意□尚可□待改進			
其他建議：			

總經銷：永續圖書有限公司

永續圖書 線上購物網
www.foreverbooks.com.tw

您可以使用以下方式將回函寄回。

您的回覆，是我們進步的最大動力，謝謝。

① 使用本公司準備的免郵回函寄回。

② 傳真電話：（02）8647-3660

③ 掃描圖檔寄到電子信箱：

yungjiuh@ms45.hinet.net